God's Warrior

by

Jessica Williams

You're are an awesome classmate and friend. Thanks for talking with me so much in English.

Jessica Williams

DORRANCE PUBLISHING CO., INC.
PITTSBURGH, PENNSYLVANIA 15222

All Rights Reserved
Copyright © 2010 by Jessica Williams
No part of this book may be reproduced or transmitted
in any form or by any means, electronic or mechanical,
including photocopying, recording, or by any information
storage and retrieval system without permission in
writing from the author.

ISBN: 978-1-4349-0387-7
Printed in the United States of America

First Printing

For information or to order additional books, please write:
Dorrance Publishing Co., Inc.
701 Smithfield St.
Pittsburgh, Pennsylvania 15222
U.S.A.
1-800-788-7654
www.dorrancebookstore.com

Chapter One:
Rakkarah

A girl stood in a large room in front of a floor-length mirror. She wore black pants and a blood-red shirt that fell slightly off her shoulders. This girl was Rakkarah, the eighteen-year-old ruler of the white witches. She swept her black hair out of her face and turned to speak to the three women standing behind her.

"I'd like to be alone for a while," she said to them.

"Alright," said the oldest of the women. "I'll be back for you soon." As the three women left the room, the girl looked back into the mirror and began to speak.

"I don't know why, but I always like to be alone before a battle. I suppose it gives me a chance to center myself. You would think that because I was born into this war, I would be used to it by now, but maybe it's one of those things that never settles on you. It might settle on those who don't have to fight, but for a warrior such as myself, the strange feeling never goes away. Even harder is when you are at the center of a war and a prophecy like I am. I'll never forget the day I found out who I was to become. I was fourteen, only a year into my training as a witch, when suddenly, my life changed forever." She fell into the memory of that unbelievable day:

She stood in a large stone room with the rest of the students and teachers, talking to her two best friends, Miya and Damon.

The day had been as normal as days ever were, and the conversations were light—although this was about to change.

"How do you think you did on the exam?" asked the blonde-haired Miya. "I probably did horribly," she said in her usual unconfident tone.

"You probably did fine. Even if you did mess up, it's not the end of the world," said Rakkarah.

"That's easy for you to say, Rakkarah. I've never seen you mess up an exam once," said Miya, laughing. At that moment, several people walked up behind the group.

"Why not just bow down and worship her, Miya? All you do is stand around and suck up to her! Well, I suppose you have to. If she left, you wouldn't have anyone to keep you from getting walked on," said the girl in the front.

"Leave her alone, Leara," warned Rakkarah.

"Why? It's true. You're so predictable, Rakkarah. You'll finish training and go off and fight for the white witches like the rest of your family," snapped Leara, whose voice revealed her hatred of white witches.

"Yeah, and you'll go join the dark ones," said Rakkarah, showing no particular emotion. Rakkarah knew what would happen; it was inevitable.

"Tell me: While you're praying to that God of yours, don't you ever wonder why He hasn't helped you win the war yet, if He's so real?" asked Leara. She was becoming very frustrated that she could not anger Rakkarah.

"We're going to win, Leara. He'll make sure we do," said Rakkarah. Leara pulled out her wand. She was going to prove she was right the only way she knew how.

"Let's see if He helps you now," Leara whispered. She brought her wand down over her head and cast a spell. The spell probably would have hit anyone else, but Rakkarah was too good of a fighter. Rakkarah pulled out her wand just in time and deflected Leara's spell, then quickly cast one of her own. The force of the spell caused Leara's feet to leave the ground, and when she landed, she passed out.

The room stood in stunned silence for a moment. Most only were shocked over the sudden fight, but five people in the room were in disbelief for a very different and darker reason. One teacher attended to Leara, while the five men and women in the corner ushered Rakkarah from the room. They arrived at the door of an abandoned room and let Rakkarah inside.

"We'll be back in a minute, Rakkarah," said one of the women, looking at Rakkarah in a way she never had before. She closed the door behind her and turned to look at the other four in disbelief.

"It's her," she said, shocked.

"Yes, I had my suspicions, but now…I'm sure," whispered an older man, whose face showed a mixture of joy and grief.

"Shall we tell her now?" asked a sandy-haired man.

"Of course not; she's fourteen. The truth will terrify her," objected another woman.

"So you propose that we let her walk blindly into what she faces? We send her to do what dozens have died trying, with no idea she's supposed to do it. We will tell her, but only what she needs to know. We can't possibly hide it from her," said the older man. He turned back to the room where Rakkarah was waiting, breathed deeply, and opened the door.

Rakkarah was sitting on a nearby table, waiting. She was surprised to see that all of the men and women had shadows of sad smiles of their faces. The older man walked forward slowly until he was about two feet away from Rakkarah. Rakkarah recognized him at once; her grandfather had known and often spoke of this aged, but very powerful, wizard.

"Rakkarah I am Larson Rice, the—" he began, but Rakkarah cut in.

"The head of the council," said Rakkarah knowingly. Larson had taken over the council two years ago.

"Yes," he said smiling. "Now, about what happened back there—" he began again.

"I'm sorry, but I couldn't do anything to stop it," she apologized.

"What happened between the two of you has a greater meaning then you know," said Larson.

"What?" asked Rakkarah, who was getting more confused by the second.

"You know all about the war, of course," said Larson. He knew that every member of Rakkarah's family was involved in the war. "So you will know how many people have tried to kill the leader of dark army."

"Over one hundred," said Rakkarah. She did not see what the war had to do with her fighting with a classmate.

"There is a reason that none of them have killed her: No one can, except for one person. At the beginning of the war, a prophecy was made about a great warrior who would come to fight. It told that the warrior would have great power, and only this one would be able to defeat the dark army. If and when the warrior kills the dark leader, all other dark warriors will die with her. The warrior is going to be the leader of our people, a princess during the war and a queen when it is finished," said Larson.

"Not that I don't find this all fascinating, but what does it have to do with me?" asked Rakkarah. Larson smiled sympathetically.

"The warrior…is you," he said.

"No, I'm no great warrior. I don't have any power that the others don't," said Rakkarah in disbelief.

"Rakkarah, no student who has come to this training house has been able to cast a spell as powerful as the one you just cast until the age of at least twenty, and some never do. Whether you think so or not, you are unnaturally powerful for your age, and you will only get more powerful," said Larson.

"Are you sure I'm the one?" asked Rakkarah. She felt the life she knew was about to end, and a new one would take its place.

"I am. You are now Princess Rakkarah," whispered Larson.

The memory of that day faded, and Rakkarah spoke again.

"Now, four years later, I still have trouble believing it. The only thing I know is that I want to destroy dark magic, and restore the good to our world. Before the war began, the mortals thought all magic was the same, and they hated us all; but now they know as well as we do that magic can be as different as day and night. White witches were born with powers. We view them as a gift from God, and we use them for good. Dark witches, however, are either white witches who rebelled, or mortals who gained powers by swearing allegiance to the dark army. They use their powers for selfish purposes and don't care how it affects others. They believe this is freedom, but, unknowingly, they are prisoners to themselves."

Someone knocked on the door. The older woman had come back.

"It's time, Kar," she said gently. Rakkarah picked up her wand from a nearby table and walked out of the room. Outside the door, the woman waited with two men. All of them had been there the day Rakkarah was told of her destiny.

"Today, I am battling Alena," thought Rakkarah. "She is a very powerful dark witch, but not the one I must defeat to destroy them all. A battle happens when one witch or wizard challenges another; I challenged her, and she accepted. If she knew my destiny, she might have thought again. Precious few know about the prophecy, so the dark witches and wizards don't know their way of life is in danger. I remind myself constantly to be as prepared as possible when I face Callise, the leader of the dark rebellion, because no part of the prophecy says I will defeat her—only that I can."

They stopped outside a pair of double doors. Just before they opened, Rakkarah whispered, "Father, be with me." The doors opened to reveal a large circular room. Alena waited in the middle of the room with four dark warriors behind her. Several other people stood by the walls. Rakkarah walked forward and stopped four feet away from Alena. In a battle, the person who was challenged picks the stakes: powers or life. If the stakes are powers, then the loser becomes a mortal; if they are life, then the battle continues until one of the warriors dies. Rakkarah wondered which she would be fighting to keep this time. She looked to her right to see Damon standing on the sidelines. He gave her a slight smile and mouthed, "Don't be nice." She smiled and mouthed back, "I won't." She looked back at Alena, who gave her an evil glare—a glare that showed all the hate the war had created. But Rakkarah's face showed no hate; it showed only weariness from fighting so many battles and taking so many lives.

A man stepped forward and began to speak. The room fell silent. It was this man's job to mediate the battles and record them for the record.

"This is the battle of Princess Rakkarah and Alena Nash. The terms will be stated now by Ms. Nash." He paused to let Alena set her terms.

"My terms are life," said Alena.

"Settled: The loser of the battle will lose her life. Death spells are permitted, due to the terms. The agreement will be preformed now." He stood back as the two witches extended their wands and said in unison, "Agreed." They both retreated a few paces, and the dull look in Rakkarah's eyes was replaced by a look of fire. They stood on edge, waiting for the signal.

"Battle!" shouted the mediator.

The women moved immediately. Rakkarah sent a spell at Alena that knocked her to the ground, and Alena retaliated with a spell that gashed Rakkarah's shoulder. Rakkarah jumped to avoid a low-aimed spell, then sent a new attack of her own. The battle raged for thirty minutes. Alena had a cut on her cheek, and Rakkarah's hand was bleeding. For a while, neither was able to gain control of the battle. A well-aimed spell hit Alena in the chest and caused her to double over. Rakkarah quickly sent a series of spells at Alena, who was in such pain she no longer could cast spells. In one last desperate attempt to regain the battle, Alena sent a very weak spell at Rakkarah, who deflected it easily. Everyone knew now that the end of the battle was here; one last spell and it would be over. Rakkarah raised her wand and pointed it at Alena.

"Lifeara exitus!" yelled Rakkarah. Alena slumped to the ground, dead. Rakkarah looked at the dark warriors who had come with Alena.

"No...she can't be. She's not..." stammered one of the girls through her tears. A white warrior gave Alena's body to one of the men. He stood, holding Alena's body, with glazed-over eyes. Everyone in the room had seen that look before—the look of a warrior who was no longer capable of fighting. They had seen it in battles many times: A warrior would be fighting one minute, and the next they would stop, staring at some unknown thing, and walk away. They had seen it happen when a warrior saw a friend or hero fall in a battle, as though the observer no longer could separate fantasy from reality.

"You have to leave. You will receive your wands at the gate," said the man who had handed over Alena's body. The four walked out, two crying, one angry, and the blank-faced warrior escorted by a few white warriors. Once the doors had closed, the white warriors began to cheer. Rakkarah gave them a soft smile.

"Thank you all, but the battle has tired me. I think I will go and rest a while," said Rakkarah. She walked out of the room calmly, but once she was out of sight of the others, she walked quickly back to her room. She closed the door behind her and sat on the window seat. Staring out of the window at the setting sun, she became lost in her thoughts, and a single tear rolled down her cheek. She was in such deep thought, she didn't notice the door open. Damon walked up behind her and put his hand on her shoulder.

"Hey, Kar," said Damon.

"Hey, Damon," said Rakkarah, slightly surprised.

"How are you?" he asked in concern.

"Fine," said Rakkarah, in a voice that showed she was far from fine.

"Why do you lie to me?" he said with a small laugh, sitting down in front of her. "I'm your best friend; you're allowed to be not alright around me." He picked up a leather-bound book sitting beside him and opened it. It was filled with pictures taken an eternity ago. It was hard to believe that they once had laughed that freely, that they once had been allowed to be young. Looking at the photos, Rakkarah sighed.

"I'd give anything to be that girl again, even for just one day. I'm nothing like I was four years ago," she said sadly.

"You are different. You're haunted: you don't laugh as much as you used to, and you won't let anyone in, not even me," said Damon softly. "But you're still the same, too. You still care for everyone, even when most people wouldn't, you're still my best friend, and—"

"Damon, don't," Rakkarah whispered. She knew what he was going to say next.

"Kar, why not? Why can't we be together?" he asked her.

"Because you'll get hurt," she said.

"I'm in the war now, too. I'm in plenty of danger," he argued.

"You've only been a warrior for six months. You've only had two battles. They don't see you as a big threat yet. I'm the person they want dead most, and they'll use anyone I care about to get to me. You're in enough danger being my best friend. If it becomes anything more, you might as well dig your grave," said Rakkarah, almost begging to stop the conversation. She couldn't deny she wanted to be with Damon, but she was not going to let him die because she couldn't hold her ground.

"Look, Kar, life isn't about how long you live, it's about what you live for. It's about what you do with the time you have. I don't want to die knowing I didn't fight for what I cared for," said Damon.

"Damon, after the war it will be—"

"We aren't promised an 'after the war'—we were promised today. Plus, this war could last another twenty years, and we can't wait that long to live our own lives. Talk to Larson. Try to find a way," said Damon. Rakkarah looked back at him, knowing he was right.

"I will," she said, smiling. At that moment, the door flew open. The same man who had walked with Rakkarah down the hall was standing breathless in the doorway. He obviously had run to the room.

"Princess, you are needed in the meeting hall—you too, Damon," he said urgently. Without hesitation, they ran down the hall.

"What happened, Brice?" asked Rakkarah. The fire that had been in her eyes during the battle had returned to its full blaze.

"I don't know. Larson said he would explain when you got there," said Brice. They burst through a door into a large room where about twenty people were standing around, looking anxious.

"Larson, what's going on?" asked Rakkarah.

"Everyone, quiet!" exclaimed Larson. Silence fell immediately, but it was a loud silence, as if the air itself said something was not right.

Chapter Two:
The Raid

"We received a tip from one of our people on the inside that the dark army is planning a mass raid tonight," said Larson. "They won't come here, but everywhere else is a target. What do you want to do, Rakkarah?" he asked.

"I want you to contact all the warriors and tell them to move their families into safe houses. Then, you tell them to station themselves for defense, but to take no unnecessary risks. They have my permission to kill on sight. And I want all those closest to me in this mansion within thirty minutes. This is revenge for Alena, so that's who they'll go for first," said Rakkarah. No one moved; all were in shock.

"Get moving!" shouted Rakkarah. They all hurried out of the room, leaving only Rakkarah, Damon, and Larson there.

"Larson, take care of things here. I'm going out there," said Rakkarah as she turned to leave the room, but she was stopped by Damon.

"Kar, if anyone needs to stay here, it's you. I'll go," said Damon.

"This is revenge on me. You'll be one of the first they look for. My warriors are not going to risk their lives if I don't risk mine," she argued.

"You can settle this after we clear up one matter first," said Larson.

"Larson, do you think now is a good time?" asked Damon.

"It's as good as any. Now Rakkarah, by now I'm sure you and Damon have talked about your relationship, and you have made a million feeble excuses why it cannot be," said Larson in his usual tone—the tone that made everything seemed so simple and uncomplicated. It always infuriated Rakkarah, because her life was exactly the opposite.

"Feeble? Larson, you can't turn a blind eye to this. You know what will happen if the dark warriors get even a hint of a relationship between Damon and me. He'll be killed," said Rakkarah. Damon was right, she thought; this was not a good time for this conversation.

"This is true, but I don't think either one of you would be foolish enough to advertise the fact to the world. It's very simple, Kar: Don't tell anyone. Callise already knows Damon is your closest friend. She knows all the important people in your life: Damon, Miya, your father, Miranda, me. The danger is already present," said Larson.

"But what if someone found out by accident?" asked Rakkarah.

"Rakkarah, your whole life is a risk—Damon's too—but the risk is not big enough to prevent your happiness," said Larson. Rakkarah looked at him, still unsure what he was saying.

"Let me ask you this: What is the point of fighting this war if you aren't fighting for something, other then just ending Callise?" asked Larson. At that point, Rakkarah finally understood what she hadn't for four years: There would be a life after the war. Words failed her, so she simply nodded. Larson left the room, leaving Rakkarah and Damon alone. Damon smiled at her.

"So you finally figured it out?" he asked her.

"Yeah, I guess I did," she answered, smiling. He walked to her and took her hand. She had always been so smart in matters of war and strategy, but blind to what she really wanted for herself. She had always come last in her mind. But for the first time in their lives, the war was not there; their own lives were first. It would have been wonderful for that feeling to last, but the next second, the reality of their lives came bursting back into the room.

"You need to go to Miya!" bellowed Brice.

"What happened?" asked Rakkarah urgently.

"Just go," said Brice. Rakkarah and Damon ran out of the room without another word. Horrible thoughts swarmed through Rakkarah's head. Miya was not a warrior. She had always been soft-spoken and timid, always afraid to fight. If Miya, who Rakkarah once had seen faint in defense class, had been forced to face a dark warrior, Rakkarah did not want to see what awaited at her destination.

They arrived ten minutes later in Miya's front yard. Rakkarah saw that the door was hanging by one of its hinges and one of the windows was broken; the sight made the air leave her lungs. She ran into the house, with Damon at her heels. They looked around and saw a shocked Miya sitting on the couch. Rakkarah hurried to her friends' side, ignoring the bowing warriors who had come to rescue Miya.

"Miya, are you alright? Who did it? Did we detain them?" asked Rakkarah, first to Miya, then to everyone else in the room.

"Kar, it's alright," said Miya.

"Who was it?" asked Rakkarah. Now that she was sure Miya was safe, her worry was being replaced by anger.

"It was Nathan Blake, Princess," said the nearest warrior.

"And did you capture him?" asked Rakkarah.

"No. He was killed," said the warrior.

"By whom?" asked Rakkarah.

"By me," said Miya.

"What?" stammered Rakkarah.

"He broke in and he started sending spells at me and…I had to," said Miya.

"Its okay, Miya," said Damon, "Let's go back to the mansion." Without another word, they set off.

When they arrived back, Miya turned to talk to Rakkarah.

"Kar, I want to be trained," said Miya.

"Absolutely not. I won't allow it," said Rakkarah.

"I'm not asking to be made a warrior, I just want to learn to fight," said Miya.

"You don't have to be a warrior to be challenged. If you are formally trained in battle, you are no longer considered a civilian, which means you would become part of the war. Do not ask me to sign your death sentence. Within these walls I can protect you, but if you step into training, I can't," said Rakkarah. She would not let another person she loved sacrifice herself in the ring of battle.

"Kar, I'm not a child; you don't have to protect me," argued Miya.

"Miya, you've never seen a battle. You don't know what it's like to see someone you love step into that circle and know they might never step out. You don't know what it's like to walk into a room and look into the eyes of a person who wants more than anything to take your life, to know that one mistake means your life is over," said Rakkarah.

"I can deal with it," proclaimed Miya. Rakkarah paused a few moments before replying.

"I'll make you a deal. You come to my next battle, and I'll have Damon watch you. If you get emotional or upset, then you don't train, but if you hold up… I'll train you myself," said Rakkarah.

"You mean it?" asked Miya.

"Yes, but for now I want you to be checked out by a doctor and get some rest. Tomorrow will be busy," said Rakkarah. Miya walked up the stairs to the doctor. Rakkarah turned to talk to Damon.

"It's going to drive me crazy to just sit here and wait, but I think I should stay here in case Miya needs me," said Rakkarah.

"She seems fine," replied Damon.

"The reality of what happened hasn't set in on her yet. About a month ago, we had a warrior win his first battle. He was happy for a few hours, but then the fact that he had killed someone hit him, and he couldn't deal with it. He went a little crazy for a while," explained Rakkarah.

"Kar, why do you feel like you have to fight every chance you get?" asked Damon. He had wondered this for a long time.

"I guess I think if I fight enough, one day I'll understand," she answered cryptically.

"Understand what?" asked Damon.

"Why the prophecy named me and not someone else. I mean, look at Larson: He's much more powerful. Why not him?" she wondered, more to herself than to Damon.

"No, Larson never could be the ruler you are, never the warrior you are," said Damon. His expression was serious, yet his eyes held the lightness that was always there when he looked at her.

"What?" asked Rakkarah. She had never once thought herself more powerful than Larson.

"There's something in you that isn't in other people, Kar—something in your eyes. I see it when you fight. It's like they pierce your opponent, like you know what they're going to do before it happens. When you want to do something, there's passion in them, and I know you won't stop until you do it. You can't find that in everybody," he said. He looked at her in a way that showed she held a special place in his heart.

"How do you do that?" she asked him.

"Do what?" he asked.

"Make me feel like I'm better than I think I am," she said.

"You are," he said, as if there were no other explanation. He leaned forward and kissed her cheek, then added, "Even if you don't see it." At that moment, Larson rounded the corner.

"I've been looking for you, Rakkarah," said Larson.

"Do we know anything yet?" she inquired urgently.

"Yes, we've killed about fifty of them. It's not quite over yet, but it should be soon," said Larson. He knew the question she would ask next—she always did, but he hated the look on her face when he gave her the answer.

"How many have we lost?" she asked.

"Seven are dead, and nine are badly injured. It's really turning out in our favor, Kar," he said, his heart breaking at the look on her face.

"That's a comforting thought, unless you're the one who caused it," she said in a hollow voice.

"Kar, they would have done this no matter who killed her. Go get some sleep; we're having a meeting at noon." She nodded silently. He put his hand on her shoulder. His next words were in an understanding, fatherly tone: "Rakkarah, you did what you had to do. None of our warriors would thank you for showing mercy to one of the most lethal, dark warriors ever known." She looked into his kind eyes and knew he was right, but it still was hard for her not to blame herself. Larson left a moment later, leaving Rakkarah and Damon alone again.

"He's right, you know," said Damon softly. She gave him a look that said, "Don't try to sugar coat it."

"They wanted revenge because I killed her. That makes it my fault," she told him in exasperation.

"Someone had to kill her, and you're the best there is," said Damon. They both began to laugh.

"Oh, thanks, I'm a great murderer," she said sarcastically.

"Well, you are. Now go up to bed. Larson is right: Tomorrow is going to be crazy," he said, still smiling. She nodded and returned to her room.

She fell onto her bed, exhausted. She fell asleep almost at once. She always slept in a light sleep; too often her nights had been interrupted by sudden screams of panic. She could not count the number of times she had awoken to being urgently summoned to the meeting hall.

She awoke the next morning before eight. She got up and walked into her bathroom to shower; as she did, her mind was filled with a wave of thought.

"At noon I will know the answers to all of the questions in the back of my mind. Who are they? Do I know them? Who killed them? What did they leave behind? The questions flash through my mind like bolts of lightning. Meetings after raids are always sad affairs. We take time to honor the fallen and pray for the wounded and all of the affected families. Then we try to focus on our next plan of action, even though our minds are somewhere else."

She dressed quickly, then walked out to sit on the window sill, as she so often did.

"I've been praying the same prayer for four years now: 'Father, give me the strength to fight and the wisdom to make the right decisions. Please keep the ones I love safe and lead me so I may win this war.' For the most part, He has given me what I have asked. I never have lost a battle. Every day I learn new things that move me closer to defeating Callise. But two who I loved dearly have fallen."

At noon Rakkarah, the council, and several warriors were shut in the meeting hall. Rakkarah stood, a Bible open in her hands. She read:

> The Lord is my shepherd, I shall not want. He makes me lie down in green pastures, He leads me beside still waters, He restores my soul. He guides me in the path of righteousness for His names sake. Yea though I walk through the valley of the shadow of death I will fear no evil for you are with me; your rod and your staff they comfort me. You prepare a table for me in the presence of mine enemies: you anoint my head with oil, my cup runs over. Surely goodness and mercy will follow me all the days of my life and I shall dwell in the house of the Lord forever.

She closed the book and looked at the people gathered before speaking again. "I know the loss of our warriors is hard, but we have the comfort of knowing they are with the Lord. The dark witches do not have that comfort about the fifty they lost. Though we lost only seven, we must remember that those lives are not a mere statistic. They were someone's children, brothers, sisters, husbands, wives. Three were mothers or fathers. Let me assure you that growing up without one of your parents is very hard." She broke off for a moment; the last sentence seemed to haunt her.

"We have to keep going. The best way to honor those who died is to make sure that their task is completed. So that means back to business. I want training increased, and no one will move out of the safe houses until I say." She was back on the topic of war, and her eyes burned again. A sandy-haired man in his early thirties spoke.

"With all respect, Princess, do you really think more training is necessary? I mean, we won fifty-to-seven; it hardly seems we're in a struggle." He spoke in an arrogant tone that clearly showed he thought Rakkarah was being ridiculous. At his words,

Rakkarah's eyes blazed in such a way that it seemed sparks would fly from them.

"We won by that large a number because they were fighting out of rage. When you fight out of rage, you take unnecessary risks; you don't think as quickly, and your wits are not as sharp. Until we can go through a raid and lose not one warrior, we need more training. Also, since you have never fought a battle in your life, you'll forgive me if I suspect you don't know what you're talking about. So, until the day you are given the right and power to question me, we will continue to do things as I see fit." She did not sound angry, but something underlying her voice made it clear she would not be addressed in that manner again.

The man looked as if he had been hit by an unexpected blow and was not sure what to do. After a full minute of staring into Rakkarah's eyes, he seemed to understand it was in his best interest not to speak again. The rest of the room was hard-pressed to contain their amusement. They found it amazing that an eighteen-year-old girl had the ability to silence a grown man with no effort at all.

"Now then," Rakkarah said, going on as if nothing had happened, "I want a list of all the dark warriors who died, and a revised list of the ones still living. I don't want anybody to issue a challenge for a few days. As I said before, if they fight out of rage, they will probably lose, and most of them will be challenging for revenge." After Rakkarah had resumed her seat, Larson stood and spoke.

"Everyone is dismissed except for the council." Rakkarah looked at Larson, and she understood he did not want her present. Without a word, she stood up and followed Damon out of the room. He gave her a puzzled look.

"Aren't you going to stay for the council meeting?" he asked.

"No. Larson doesn't want me there," she said simply.

"I didn't think he could keep you out of the council meetings," said Damon.

"He can't," she said. When Damon continued to look at her curiously, she went on. "Larson keeps little from me, and when he does, it's for a good reason. He'll tell me when I need to know."

"Why is it that you will question anybody in the world but him?" Damon asked. After years of experience with Rakkarah, he had learned never to try to keep anything from her. In fact, no one was able to keep her in the dark about anything for long.

"I don't know. I guess it's because he was the one who told me everything—well, everything I needed to know. He's been with me since day one of all this, and I've just never felt the need to know anything more then he chooses to tell me. I can't explain it," she said.

"You still don't know the whole prophecy?" asked Damon.

"No. About a year ago, Larson offered to give it to me. I was in my room, and he walked in with the paper in his hand. He said there was good in knowing and good in not, and it was time I decided what good I wanted to take," said Rakkarah, who had gone off into a slightly dreamlike state.

"So you said no? You saw it right in front of you, and you said no? How?" asked Damon, who knew very well that if he were offered a look into his future, he would not be able to resist for more than five minutes.

"It took me three days and a lot of talks with Larson and God to decide. In the end, I knew it would drive me out of my mind. Damon, can you imagine knowing the signs that will come before my last battle? I always would be looking for a sign—anybody would. I never could have had another peaceful moment if I had read what was on that scroll," she said, as if wanting him to confirm that she was not insane for passing up the opportunity.

"You're right. But what was it like to see the prophecy in front of you?" he asked her.

"Strange—and scary. I just couldn't believe that my future was shown on that old piece of paper. It was strange knowing that before I was even born, people were thinking about me, and even if they didn't know who I was, they knew who I would be. It was scary, because even though I knew there was a prophecy, something about seeing it made it seem more real than it ever had before," she explained. She never had talked about this to anyone before, but she was glad she was telling Damon.

"So will he still let you see it if you change your mind?" he asked.

"I knew there would be times it would drive me crazy, now that I had seen it. I was afraid I would give in to the temptation one day, so I made Larson swear that he wouldn't let me see it again. I just can't risk losing the war over my curiosity," said Rakkarah, showing the wisdom beyond her years that made so many admire her.

"I don't think I could have said no," said Damon. Rakkarah's ability to leave things to destiny was one of the traits her admired most in her.

"I almost said yes, but…I remembered something my grandfather always used to say," she said, smiling at the memory of the old man who had been her hero.

"What did he say?" Damon asked.

"'If God had meant for you to know how your life was going to work out, He would have sent you with a biography,'" she said with a laugh.

"Funny, but true," said Damon, who also had been very fond of him.

"I need to find Dad. I haven't had the chance. It's been so—" She stopped, because as they rounded the corner, her father stood waiting. Rakkarah was the female image of her father. The same dark hair, the same nose—but what made the resemblance so remarkable were the eyes. Just like his daughter's, William's eyes held a burning fire. The same had been true of her grandfather.

"Kar, thank God. You didn't go out there, did you?" said her father as he rushed toward his daughter.

"Calm down, Dad. There was a big raid because of my battle with Alena, and yes, I went out there to get Miya," she said.

"Why on earth would you go out there? It's a miracle that a hundred of them didn't swarm you the second you walked out the door," scolded her father.

"Because going out there is my job. Why do you insist on treating me like a child?" she said, not able to contain a small smile.

"Because you are my child, warrior or not," he said, also smiling as he embraced his daughter. He couldn't believe how strong she had become, stronger than anyone should ever have to be.

"I have to go see to some things. I'll see you later on. I love you, sweetheart," he said.

"I love you too, Dad," said Rakkarah. The war had taught her never to miss the chance to tell people she loved them, just in case it was the last time she saw them.

Rakkarah and Damon set off to find Miya. Nothing in particular was troubling them, but that was not the case for all of their friends. If Rakkarah knew what was happening, she would have felt very differently.

Chapter Three:
The First Sign

Larson sat in the meeting hall with two men and two women. When he raised his head to speak, it was in a voice of attempted strength.

"You all know what the raid meant as well as I do. Now, we have to make a difficult decision," he said, looking around at each of them.

"Larson, maybe this isn't the raid," said one of the women hopefully.

"Do you really believe that? I know you don't want to, but is there any doubt in your mind that this is the raid we have waited for?" asked Brice sympathetically.

"I know, but…Why now?" she asked, as if the question had a logical answer.

"It's not right now; it's just the first sign. The prophecy says that after this raid, Rakkarah will have fifty more battles along with three more signs, then her battle with Callise."

"That's no sign of time. Those signs and battles could happen in a month," she said, irritated.

"And it could be five years. The prophecy says the princess will have a battle that causes a raid, which will yield great loss for the dark army. No previous raid has cost them so many, Miranda. It then names the three signs: the past will give her hope, the past will haunt her, and a fire will burn to its full blaze," said Larson.

When he had started to speak, his voice had been strong, but by the end, it had become slow and weak.

"Now, we need to decide if we should tell Rakkarah the prophecy or not. I have always said I would tell her when she needed to know. A year ago, I offered the information, but she declined. Now I don't know if it's the right time to tell her or not. I don't want her to anticipate what's next, to count every battle, to think she sees signs when they are not there. She is strong, level-headed, and a great warrior, but she is also a young girl, and a lot of people tend to forget that," said Larson.

After a moment, Brice spoke. "Understand, I say this not because I want to keep Rakkarah from the truth, but take it as you will. I think Rakkarah performs best when she doesn't have to dwell on things for long periods of time. If she knows how the prophecy ends, she'll have time to think about the worst-case scenario; it's only human nature. I mean, honestly, we're all worrying and thinking about the 'what ifs,' and we're not the ones facing the battle. What do you think that would do to Rakkarah? What would it do to any of us if we were told that the countdown to the battle had begun—the battle that could end our lives and decide the fate of everyone we love? Fifty battles would go by as fast as fifty seconds. For her own good, we should let her walk this road without interference." He stopped talking; he had said what needed to be said. Every face in the room showed the same expression. All of them knew this was for the best.

After several minutes of silence, Larson spoke. "So, we agree to not tell her?" They all nodded. One man put his head in his hands. The next man seemed to be going over all of the possibilities in his mind, wondering if they had made the right decision. The woman named Miranda was staring straight ahead, as if unsure of what she had just done, while tears were falling down the other woman's face. But Larson was unreadable. His face showed one thousand different emotions combined into one expression.

"Well, I guess that's everything," he whispered, as if he couldn't think of anything else to say. His voice had a sound of finality, sealing the agreement that just had been made. Everyone filed out of the room, but he stayed. When the door had closed, he started to pray. His voice was tired and desperate. It was the voice of a man who had traveled the road of war and secrets for too long.

"Lord, I don't understand this. Since the beginning of the war, I have given my life to ending it. It was my job to find Rakkarah, to look for the signs, and to put her into the final battle. Now that the time is here, it is the last thing I want to do. I have become so close to her, and you ask me to throw her into the lion's den. She is a wonderful girl, and she deserves a life free from murder. She was made to kill when she was barely sixteen, and now, at eighteen, you put the weight of the world on her shoulders. Lord, I would rather live in this war until my dying day than see her die. She is so strong, but how much can she stand? Every day she lives with the knowledge that if she dies, everyone she loves will become slaves to the dark witches. Every day she has to contemplate that if she falls, your Word will be taken from us, and anyone found worshipping you will die. How can she stand it? Lord, if you cannot take this burden from her, then please, guide her through it. Give her peace, and allow her to defeat those who oppose you. Father, please keep my girl safe. Amen." In the course of the prayer, tears had begun to fall from his eyes. Now, as he looked up, he saw he was not alone.

"I thought you left," he said to Miranda.

"I did. I came back," said Miranda, who was also teary-eyed.

"I'm sorry. I shouldn't keep falling apart like this, but..." Larson trailed off.

"I know, you love Kar. We all love her, but you're the one who is closest to her," said Miranda understandingly. She had wanted Larson to talk about this for a long time. She worried about him, always keeping his emotions away from the world.

"I see that look, Miranda. I don't want to talk about mine or anybody else's attachment to Rakkarah," he said in a voice that showed he was finished with the conversation. Unfortunately for him, Miranda wasn't. He had never been able to make her drop a subject, so he didn't know why he was trying now. Even when they were children, he always had been unable to deter her. It was one of the things that he loved—and hated—about her. She also was the one person who always could tell what was going through his head. It amazed him how much his little sister knew about him.

"Larson, you need to learn there is a difference between being strong and being isolated," said Miranda, walking forward and putting her hand on his shoulder.

"I just don't like sharing my weakness with the world," he said, irritated. Why did she always want to talk about his emotions? It was what he liked to talk about least. He remembered a time when he had felt safe to say how he felt, but that time had gone thirty years ago when the war had started. Of course, he never had liked to appear weak, but now, just loving someone could earn them death. One of the people who knew that best was Rakkarah. She had lost more than just her freedom and childhood to this war. No, he would not think about that. No one liked to think about that.

"Larson, do you know what today is?" she asked him. She had done it again, brought up exactly what he wanted to avoid.

"Of course, November twenty-third," he whispered, as though it were a dagger through his heart. Six years ago today, Rakkarah's grandfather had been murdered. Then, two years later, on the very same day, Rakkarah's mother had disappeared. Larson looked into his sister's eyes.

"I miss him," said Larson, unable to stop himself.

"I know. We all do," she said quietly.

"I never thought he could be taken. He was our leader, and the best warrior who ever lived, other then Rakkarah. He was my dearest friend," he said. His voice showed that tears were not enough to express this grief.

"You can't avoid this conversation with her forever. She has her own ideas of what happened, and you should know leaving loose ends can be dangerous," said Miranda. They both knew this subject had not been discussed with Rakkarah as it needed to be. It all had happened before Rakkarah had been named princess, so it had been watered down to coincidence by most of the community. Only the council, Rakkarah, and those close to her had seen it for what it really was. As far as anyone knew, Rakkarah had not spoken about her thoughts on the matter to anybody. This was strange, because Rakkarah usually never withheld anything from Larson or her father. It was also Larson's unwillingness to discuss the matter that made it a taboo topic around the mansion.

"I'm sure Rakkarah is smart enough to know what really happened," said Larson defiantly. Why did he not want to talk about this with Miranda? They talked about everything together. Perhaps opening the wound of losing Aaron and Isabella was something he was not sure he could handle. He knew he was not going to win this battle with his sister, so he decided to compromise. "Look, if she comes to me about it, then fine. But I'm not bringing it up. I think she might have forgotten that it's today anyway," he said with only a slight glimmer of hope.

Back in Rakkarah's room, the three friends were still talking, remembering funny stories from their past. After Rakkarah had talked with Miya and Damon for a while, she suddenly felt like being alone. Quite suddenly, she found an excuse to leave the room.

"Look, the next meeting is not until tonight, so I'm going to train," she said.

"Kar, we don't have training until tomorrow," said Damon, looking puzzled.

"Not that training," she said, and without pausing to explain, she turned and left. She arrived a few minutes later in a large room. It was empty, except for a few punching bags. She wrapped her hands and walked over to the big bag hanging in the middle of the room. For a moment, she stood there with no expression on her face, but in a second that all changed. As though a fire had started, rage seemed to engulf her, and she began to hit the bag with all of her strength. Larson had been wrong; she had not forgotten what day it was.

"No one says it, but everyone is thinking the same thing: the reason no one wanted me to fight last night, and the reason I rushed my family within the safety of these walls. Everyone, including me, thought that history might repeat itself," she thought as she punched relentlessly. "The death of my grandfather was one of the worst times of my life. He was the head of the council before Larson. He was challenged by Warren, the second in command over the dark army. My grandfather had the upper hand in the battle, when one of the newer dark warriors decided to turn the tables. He shot a spell at my grandfather, and when he deflected it, Warren cast the death spell. The new warrior was put to death for causing my grandfather to fall, but no one could prove what Warren had done, so he was set free. The only thing I know is that no warrior ever would perform an action like that unless their commander had told them to do so. And then there is the mystery that has plagued my thoughts for four years. What happened to my mother? Nothing about her disappearance has made sense. She simply went out for the day and never came back. The only logical explanation is that she was abducted and murdered—but a challenge never was recorded. It is rare that either side randomly murders. Unless she met a dark warrior and a fight had broken out. However, what I question the most is that her body was never returned. Returning the bodies of the fallen is the one kindness that our two sides give to each other. There was no reason not to do it then. For some reason, I never have accepted the fact that she is dead. This thought I have never spoken to anyone but God. I ask Him often to give me the closure I need and to allow me to find out what really happened." She stopped her relentless attacks on the bag. She took a step back, and then, with the quickness of lightning, she kicked it one last time. She knelt down and rested her head in her hands. She did not know it, but Damon, Miya, and her father had been watching her from the window of the room above.

"Why is she training in mortal fighting?" asked Miya.

"She thinks the best way to defeat the enemy is to know how to do what they can't. She has a point. Warriors have broken their wands in battle and were left defenseless," said Rakkarah's father.

"Let's go. She really doesn't like people watching her train," said Damon. The other two nodded, and they left the upper room. A few minutes later, Rakkarah got up and left too. She walked down the hallway and up to her room, where she found Damon and Miya waiting for her.

"Hey guys," she said, slightly out of breath.

"How was training?" asked Miya.

"Good. Let me go clean up. I'll be back in a minute," said Rakkarah. She walked back into her bathroom to take a quick shower.

As she did, she began to think about Damon and Miya: "I really don't know what I'd do without them. These last few years have been hard on them as well as on me. Most people would not put up with a friend who was distant and withdrawn for long periods of time, as I have been. Most people would abandon someone who could cost them their lives, but not them. Despite all of the pain and problems, they've stood by me. I think they stand by me even closer than before." She got out of the shower and used her wand to dry her hair.

"But, I guess I'm not the only one who has changed," she thought. "I remember a time when we all had so many dreams, a time when we thought we could do anything. Back then, if someone had told me that Damon would give up writing for war, I wouldn't have believed it.. I never would have thought it was possible for sweet, timid Miya to commit murder. I always knew I would fight. After all, war is in my blood. But, I did have other dreams. I had wanted to be a teacher at the training center, but those days are gone." She walked back into her room to sit with her two friends.

"That was fast," said Damon. Rakkarah had not been gone even ten minutes.

"I try not to take a long time anymore," said Rakkarah.

"Why?" asked Miya curiously.

"Because every other day someone comes bursting in here saying I need to come to the meeting hall. After that happened a few times, I just tried to make sure I was out as quickly as possible. It tends to be awkward when that happens," said Rakkarah. Miya and Damon both began to laugh.

"I think that would speed me up as well," said Miya through her laughter.

"So, how was training?" asked Damon.

"It was fine," said Rakkarah.

"Kar, do you think you're going to have to fight without magic?" asked Miya. Rakkarah paused a moment before answering.

"I don't know. Mortal fighting never has been used in battle, but it's not illegal. I just want to make sure I can do something she won't expect me to know how to do," said Rakkarah.

"Why has no one used it before? Why doesn't everyone know how to fight both ways?" asked Miya. To most, this answer was obvious, but Miya usually preferred not to know the details of battle.

"They don't see the need. Most people don't think there will be a time when they won't be able to use their wands. Plus, you can find few witches and wizards who think that pure strength stands a chance against magic," explained Damon.

"In truth, it doesn't, unless you know what you're doing. And even then it's hard. But I'm willing to learn, even if it probably won't work," said Rakkarah.

"Are you going to teach that to me, too, if you train me?" asked Miya.

"I will if you want me to, but you still have to prove to me you can withstand training before we worry about that," said Rakkarah.

"Get ready to prove yourself, Miya. You've been challenged, Rakkarah," said Brice in a grave tone. He had entered the room without any of them noticing. She looked behind him and saw the whole council standing in the doorway.

"Who is it, Brice?" whispered Rakkarah.

"Raiden Crain," he answered.

"When?" she whispered, even softer than before.

"Eight o'clock tonight. Do you accept?" he asked her. She looked back at the council. After a minute, she found her voice.

"Yes," she said, her voice now determined.

"No!" Damon was on his feet. "Larson, you can't let her—not today." Damon had remembered the significance of this day, just as Rakkarah and Larson had. Larson looked into Rakkarah's eyes. At the moment, he saw glowing embers, but he knew her black eyes would soon hold enough fire to destroy a city.

"It's her call, Damon," said Larson.

"Please bring my father to me. When he gets here, I want to speak to him, Larson, and Miranda privately. Damon and Miya can stay too. And please tell Gwen I need a set of clothes for the battle," said Rakkarah. Her voice held no emotion, and her expression was blank. They all left to do what she asked. Larson and Miranda sat down by the window. They both thought this was strange. Rakkarah usually liked to be alone as much as possible before a battle. They could not understand why she suddenly wanted an audience of five people, with only a few hours left before the battle.

Chapter Four:
Cheating Death

Ten minutes later, William entered the room along with Gwen, who was holding a set of Rakkarah's battle clothes. After Gwen left the room, William turned to face his daughter.

"Rakkarah, what's wrong?" asked her father.

"I was challenged. I think we all know what is going to happen tonight. All signs point to my assassination," said Rakkarah matter-of-factly.

"Surely not! You have too much security," said Miya, once again showing her ignorance of what people were willing to do in war.

"Today is not a normal day. Two were not taken from me on this day by mere coincidence. The chances are—" Rakkarah paused to control a sob that threatened to escape her throat. "—they will try to take me like they took my grandfather." They all looked as though they had seen a ghost. For an instant, in hearing her talk about him, it was as though Aaron had appeared before them.

"Then we call off the battle," said William, his rage matched only by Rakkarah's.

"Dad, I've already accepted. I will not let fear of trickery keep me from doing my job. The battle will be fought as planned," said Rakkarah.

"I have lost my father and my wife to this war and this day. I do not intend to let it take my daughter," he said, almost yelling.

"Mom didn't die in a battle, and there are precautions to take that we didn't use in Grandpa's battle. This war is my life and my job, and I intend to end it so I can have a life of my own," said Rakkarah, her voice hollow.

"Precautions may not be enough. Why will it hurt to wait one day?" argued William.

"I'm not saying I won't get hurt. I probably will; Raiden is a good fighter. But I'm not going to hide and let them think that I'm afraid of them or afraid of a day. Grandpa wouldn't have turned this battle down, and neither would you, so don't ask me to do what you yourself couldn't." Rakkarah had sounded angry at first, but by the end her voice had softened. William looked back into Rakkarah's eyes; he knew she was right.

"So, what precautions can we take, Larson?" asked William.

"I'll put a blocking spell around the ring. No one will be able to try to kill Rakkarah, except for Raiden," said Larson, trying to encourage William. Even he didn't know why he was saying this. No one could have given a better excuse to postpone the start of the fifty-battle countdown, but interfering with the plans of God never did anyone any good.

"Are you positive it will work?" questioned William.

"Completely. We can go set it up now. There are two hours left until the battle. Do you want to be alone, Kar?" asked Larson, as though he had read her mind.

"Yes, please," she whispered. Larson and Miranda both hugged her and left the room quickly. William held on to her tightly, and when he finally let go, Rakkarah saw his eyes were red with tears.

"I love you, Dad," Rakkarah said.

He managed to smile weakly at her. "I love you, too," he said softly, and then walked out.

Miya was looking scared and confused at how quickly everything had happened. Rakkarah took her hand. "You'll see," Rakkarah said simply. Miya hugged her quickly and followed William out of the room. Now, Rakkarah and Damon were left alone.

"Why are you going through with this?" asked Damon.

"It's my job," said Rakkarah, not at all in the mood to go through her reasons again.

"You can fight tomorrow, when—" Damon began, but Rakkarah cut in.

"I have never turned down a battle before, and I don't intend to start now," she said. "Kar, I care about you too much to let you practically commit suicide. What do you think it will do to the people if they lose you on the same day they lost their last leader? I can't take it, especially not today. I loved your mom and grandfather like my own family. This day haunts me, and to lose you on this day would kill me," said Damon. Rakkarah walked forward and took his hand.

"Damon, who said you were going to lose me? I'm not planning on dying. And what do you think it will do to the people if they found out I refused a battle and hid in this mansion after the dark army just killed some of our warriors? If I show fear, they will too. I can't do that to them," said Rakkarah gently.

"I know," said Damon. He knew that she was right; she always was. "I'll be there when you step in, and when you step out. Just be careful."

"I always am," said Rakkarah. He hugged her tightly, then left the room. Rakkarah walked over to the window so she could watch the gate and think for a while.

"Most will think me crazy to fight on a day that has shed so much of my family's blood, but the truth is I would have it no other way. I refuse to live in fear, and I will show them that no one else will fall on this day. Will I be hurt? Most likely. Larson's spell will not protect me from everything. This war is like a rope around my neck that threatens to strangle me. The battles are like bars on a jail cell. Only when I battle Callise will my sentence be served. Strange that I feel my freedom is so near." Rakkarah saw five dark warriors approach the gates. The guards checked them for concealed weapons and took the wand of all the warriors, except Raiden. Several men came out and escorted them into the mansion.

"I can smell their evil mixed with the putrid scent of hate," thought Rakkarah. At the moment, the moon and stars shine white. By the end of the night, their beams will reflect red on the spilled blood of a warrior." A knock on the door signaled it was time for the battle. Rakkarah opened the door to find Miranda and Brice waiting for her.

"Are you ready, Rakkarah?" asked Brice.

"Yes," said Rakkarah. They walked down the hall in silence. Rakkarah prayed for strength. The doors opened to the usual sight: warriors and the council standing by the walls, the mediator and the opponent standing in the middle, the dark warriors behind them. Rakkarah saw Miya was looking scared. She looked at Damon, who was looking at Raiden; if looks could kill, Rakkarah would not have needed to battle. She saw her father, his pain apparent: hate in his eyes for the man who was seeking to kill the one he loved above everything, and sadness that his sweet, beloved daughter was forced into this life of torture. It was because of all her loved ones that Rakkarah blazed the way she did. She knew all of them were in danger, but she was not going to allow them to be hurt. Her mind was on one thing: finishing the battle as quickly as possible.

The mediator stepped forward to start the battle. "This is the battle of Princess Rakkarah and Raiden Crain. The terms will be set by the princess." The dark warriors had always refused to call Rakkarah "Princess." This caused all of the white witches and wizards to call her Princess as much as possible while in the presence of their enemies.

"Princess, state your terms now," the mediator said.

"Life," said Rakkarah. This caused a few worried looks, but most smiled proudly. They knew their leader would never leave a dark warrior in half-existence.

"Perform the agreement," said the mediator. Rakkarah and Raiden extended their wands and said, "Agreed." The mediator stated the rules of the fight and then yelled, "Battle!" They sprang into action. A few spell were cast, but none of them made contact. Raiden sent a spell at Rakkarah that had enough force to knock her to the ground. She looked back into Raiden's eyes and gave a small smile.

"Bad choice," said Rakkarah. She began to send spells at Raiden. His attack seemed to have infused Rakkarah with the speed of lightning and the power of exploding dynamite. Raiden was unable to get off another spell. He panicked, cast his wand away, and ran toward Rakkarah. She stopped him with the shout of one final spell.

"Lifera exitus!" He fell dead at her feet. Applause broke out, and people began to cheer, but they stopped when one of the dark wizards began to shout.

"Did revenge for your family taste sweet? Enjoy it while you can. You all stand so proud behind your beloved princess, but she will fall at the feet of a dark warrior. She will fall to me!" he shouted. In his hand was Raiden's discarded wand. He attempted to send a death spell at her, but Larson's shield protected Rakkarah. A fight broke out in the audience. Damon, Larson, and William ran forward and attempted to get Rakkarah out of the room. They almost had made it to the door when Rakkarah felt something hit her in the back, followed by horrible pain. Damon and William, who each had a hold on Rakkarah's arms, felt her fall. Looking down, they saw the reason. The handle of a blade was sticking out of Rakkarah's back. She felt herself being picked up and carried out of the room. Then she fainted.

She heard muttering. The room was dark. She could feel herself lying in bed. She tried to open her eyes, but it seemed impossible. What had happened? The last thing she remembered was trying to get out of the room. She could now hear some of the whispered conversation.

"It's amazing it didn't kill her." "How long is she going to be out of battle?" "When is she going to wake up?" She recognized those voices.

"Now," she said, finally opening her eyes. Damon was sitting by her bed, pale with worry. Miya was crying. On her other side was her father, his eyes bloodshot. Larson and Miranda stood at the end of her bed. They all looked up when she spoke. She tried to sit up, but her father held her down.

"No, don't get up. You're still weak," he said.

"Are you hurting? The doctor said you might be sore for a while," said Miranda.

"Just a little stiff. What happened?" Rakkarah asked.

"You were stabbed. One of the dark warriors conjured a blade and threw it, hoping it would kill you. They knew the spell wouldn't work," said Damon.

"Did we get them?" asked Rakkarah.

"We apprehended all of them. We thought you might want to question them yourself before we dealt with them," said Larson. They all knew that by "dealt with," he meant "put to death."

"Yes, I would. How long was I out?" she asked.

"Several hours. It's almost six," said William.

"Were any of our people hurt?" asked Rakkarah.

"No, but they're outraged. They were all begging me to order a raid if you weren't awake by ten," said Larson.

"They know I don't allow raids," sighed Rakkarah.

"I know. You rest. Miranda and I need to go tell everyone that you're awake. William, you need to come too. We're going to have to put in more security measures around the safe houses," said Larson. After saying goodbye, the three of them left the room.

Rakkarah looked over at Miya. "Miya, stop crying. I'm fine," she said.

"Kar, you are not fine. You almost died. How can you expect me not to get upset?" asked Miya.

"Look, I don't need anyone to tell me that blade was about an inch from my heart. But I'm not dead; I'm alive, therefore I'm fine. Miya I saw you fall apart ten minutes into the battle when I was winning. You can't expect me to let you train. You've shown you can do what you have to when you have to, but the less you have to, the better—trust me," said Rakkarah. Miya nodded.

"I don't know how you do it," said Miya. Rakkarah smiled and took her hand.

"Because I know I have to," she said simply.

"How much longer do you think this is going to last?" asked Miya, as if hoping Rakkarah could pull out a calendar with the marked date.

"Not long. Now you go rest. We'll talk more later," said Rakkarah. Miya nodded and left the room.

"Are you alright?" asked Damon.

"I'm fine. I'm more worried about you," said Rakkarah.

"I'm fine, but when I saw you tonight, when they were healing you, you looked barely alive," said Damon.

"We won't have to live like this much longer," she said soothingly.

"How do you know? It's been thirty years. We've never lived out of war," said Damon. It was true. All eighteen years of their lives had been spent hearing the words of war: death, battle, recruitment, and raid. Their childhoods had been filled with midnight flees to safe houses and waiting in back rooms while the people they loved witnessed or participated in battles. She was trying to figure out how to explain how she knew, when Miya reentered the room.

"Yeah, how do you know, Kar?" she asked.

"I thought you were going to bed," said Rakkarah.

"I was, but I was thinking about you in here, and I got worried," said Miya.

"Thanks, Miya," said Rakkarah. They sat in silence for a while.

Rakkarah slipped into a quiet musing. "For what Miya lacks in the strength of war, she makes up for with the strength of her heart," she thought. "She is, without a doubt, the most loving and caring person I know. I so wish to be like her, but I know I can't. Being a warrior, I still love, still care. My heart has not gone completely cold, but there is a chill that was not there four years ago."

"I can't explain how I know, but something feels different," she said aloud. "It's like everything I'm doing is starting to lead up to the main event. The dark warriors' actions are changing, too. It seems like they're getting desperate. Callise wants to finish me soon, and she's trying everything. It won't be long before she decides to do it herself."

"She won't be able to," said Damon.

"She has the ability. There's no use in pretending she doesn't," said Rakkarah.

"I didn't say she can't; I said she won't," he said with a slight laugh.

"How do you know she won't?" asked Rakkarah. She smiled, but sadly. No one on earth knew who would win the battle. Everyone was so sure of her, but she wasn't.

"Because I trust God's judgment. He allowed you to be our leader because He knew you could do what no one else could. He knew He could give you the power and trust you to use it like He wanted. I know He won't allow us to be ruled by anyone except the one He chooses," said Damon. She heard his words, and they made sense, but she would never allow herself to give over completely to the belief that she would win.

"Damon is right, Kar. Trust God, and don't worry," said Miya.

"Oh yeah, the fate of the world is about to be decided. What am I worried about?" she said sarcastically, and they all laughed.

"I don't understand something: Why didn't Callise ever figure out there was a prophecy? I mean, all of a sudden a fourteen-year-old becomes princess when there never has been one before. Did it not occur to her that something was going on?" Damon asked.

"It would have, if we had allowed it to," said Rakkarah.

"What do you mean?" asked Miya.

"There's a spell; it allows us to alter knowledge," said Rakkarah.

"I don't get it," said Damon.

"We installed false knowledge into everyone's heads that my family had once ruled as I do now, and that the council decided to reinstate the monarchy. Then we put in that my father had refused the title, so it was passed down to me. The story we implanted was much more complex, but you get the picture," said Rakkarah, as if she had just explained something as simple as the sky being blue.

"But if you can do that spell, then how do you know Callise hasn't used it already?" asked Damon, who suddenly looked like he was wishing he had a shield for his mind.

"The person who invents a spell can put limits on it; they can control what it's used for. This spell has two limits. One is that it can be used only by the council, and the other is that it can be used only to help things along that are already supposed to happen, like the prophecy," explained Rakkarah.

"Then why do we know the truth?" asked Miya.

"I chose for you to know," said Rakkarah. They sat in silence for a few minutes, then Damon asked another question.

"If you can put limits on a spell, then why didn't the person who invented the death spell put a limit on it?" asked Damon.

"Do you honestly think anyone who made a spell for death would want to control it? Especially considering who made it," said Rakkarah.

"Who made it?" asked Miya.

"The first witch to christen herself a dark witch, the first rebel, the founder of this war, Callise herself," said Rakkarah, her voice haunted.

"Why didn't she put a limit on it that said only a dark warrior could use it?" asked Damon.

"Before I became a warrior, did you ever think I could kill?" asked Rakkarah.

"No," said Damon.

"What about my dad? Larson? Miranda? You? Miya? Did you ever think that they would raise their wands to take someone's life?" she continued.

"Of course not," he replied.

"Neither did she," said Rakkarah.

She then grew quiet again. "This was exactly why Callise never thought to put a limit on her spell," she thought. "She never suspected that any of us who follow God would ever utter the words 'lifera exitus.' She soon realized how wrong she was. To her, murder is sport or motivation for people to join her. She saw it only as a path to get her way. She never dreamed that someone else would use it against her and her people. Too late, she realized that both sides would use it to fight this war." They stayed awake for another hour talking before falling asleep where they sat. They awoke a few hours later to find several more people standing in the room. William, Larson, Miranda, and Gwen were all staring out of the window, smiling. Gwen looked around and saw them awake.

"It seems your people want to see their princess," said Gwen to Rakkarah. The three of them got up and walked over to the window. What Rakkarah saw melted her heart. Outside the walls were her people, at least one thousand.

"They started coming about an hour ago," said Larson.

"Gwen, get my clothes ready, please. I'm going down there," said Rakkarah.

"Are you sure you're alright?" asked Miranda.

"I'm fine. It's lying in that bed all day that will make me feel bad," said Rakkarah. She walked into the bathroom with Gwen so she could change.

"I tried to find something that would be loose on where the blade hit," said Gwen.

"Thanks. It is still a little sore," said Rakkarah. Gwen had been Rakkarah's helper for four years, but she had become a wonderful friend as well.

"Do you know when you are going to question the prisoners?" asked Gwen.

"Later today, but I doubt it will do any good. They usually won't betray Callise. They are as loyal to her as those outside are to me," said Rakkarah.

"It's easy to follow a leader who is telling you what you want to hear, but when someone tells you what you need to hear, it gets difficult. It's then you know you have a real leader," said Gwen.

"Especially when the one telling you what you need to hear nearly gets herself killed in an attack she knew was coming," said Rakkarah as Gwen fixed her hair.

"They won't turn from you. You've given them hope, and they know, as I do, that you will lead us through this. The question is, do you know?" said Gwen, smiling. They walked back into the room to rejoin the others.

"Ready?" Rakkarah asked the rest. They walked out of the room and down the hall.

"Larson, when we come back I want to question the four that accompanied Raiden Crain," said Rakkarah.

"Will nothing distract you from business?" asked Larson chidingly.

"Has it ever?" asked Miya.

"Good point," said Larson.

"I just want to get everything done while I have time," said Rakkarah, laughing with the others. They reached the front doors and walked outside. When the people realized who was walking toward them, they let out deafening cheers. After several minutes, the crowd calmed so Rakkarah could speak.

"Your loyalty surpasses anything I could ever hope for. I know the day will come when I will stand before you to proclaim that this was is over, but until that day comes, I know you will stay just as strong as you are today. I cannot promise you it will all be over tomorrow, but I can promise you that with every second I live, I will be using every breath I take to try to free you. Soon, I will be questioning the dark warriors involved in last night's events in hope that they may offer insight to the current happenings of Callise and her people. With any luck, we may learn the next moves of the dark army." The rest of her words were drowned out by a second wave of cheers.

Larson then stepped up. "Thank you, but the princess must now go to the questioning," he said. As they walked back up the path, the people began to shout again, but this time it was statements of hate for the dark army.

"Make them pay!"

"They deserve no mercy!"

As she heard the shouts, Rakkarah turned back. She raised her hand for silence.

"Do not hate them. Hate what they do. That we do not hate our enemies sets us apart from them. Not one of us here deserved mercy from God, but we all received it," she said. The crowd stood, knowing she was right. If they hated, if they wanted death for others, what separated them from those they were fighting?

All were silent for a moment, then a young man began to speak. "Our Father who art in heaven, hallowed be thy name," Slowly everyone joined in, speaking the words they had known since childhood. "Thy kingdom come, thy will be done, on earth as it is in heaven. Give us this day our daily bread, and forgive us our debts, as we forgive our debtors. And lead us not into temptation, but deliver us from evil." When the prayer was finished, Rakkarah smiled and walked back into the mansion.

"You have a way with them. You seem to be able to humble and empower them all at once," said Miranda.

"All I do is let someone who knows better than me speak through me," said Rakkarah. Miranda never could help but be amazed at Rakkarah's faith. If anyone had a reason to give up hope, she did, but she stood just as strong as ever. Her fire never went out.

They walked down a long, dark hall that lead to a place that none of them liked. They turned the corner to see two guards standing at a door, a door that could only be opened by certain people. Only Rakkarah, the council, and a select few others could enter and leave the room freely. This is where prisoners were kept, questioned, and many times, killed. As they approached, the guards stepped aside. Rakkarah put her hand on the doorknob and, after stopping a moment, opened the door. It was a large room with five doors on the back wall: the holding chambers. Three men had been sitting at a table in deep discussion, but at the sight of Rakkarah, they jumped to their feet.

"What news of the captives?" asked Rakkarah.

"Three of them are predictable, one is surprising," said one of the men.

"What do you mean?" asked Miranda.

"Well, we asked if any of them would offer up any information. Three of them refused, but one said she wants to talk. We had to remove her from the room with the other three at that point. They started beating her when she said it," said another man.

"Take me to her," said Rakkarah.

"Rakkarah, we'll wait out here. She might be reluctant to talk in front of so many people," said Larson.

"Good idea," said Rakkarah, and she walked into the room.

"Larson, don't you want to know what's happening?" asked Damon.

"I will know," said Larson.

"How?" asked Damon.

"We'll look through the wall," he said, as though it were the simplest thing in the world. He pulled out his wand and traced a large circle on the wall. The next moment, the wall vanished.

"Wow! But can't they see us, too?" asked Miya.

"No, it works like a two-way mirror. To anyone in that room, it looks like solid wall," said Larson. Inside the room, Rakkarah was walking toward a woman with lank hair and many bruises. She seemed not to know someone had entered the room. Her head was hung, and she was shaking slightly.

"I was told you have some things you wish to tell me," said Rakkarah. The girl glanced up, then threw herself at Rakkarah's feet.

"Get up. We bow before only one, and it's not me," said Rakkarah. The girl then spoke.

"After all the times I said it and never believed I would, I now bow down to the great Rakkarah." The girl looked up, and Rakkarah looked into the face of someone she had not seen for four years.

Chapter Five:
A Change of Heart

"Leara," said Rakkarah, astounded. Everything about her had changed; it was no wonder that Rakkarah had not recognized her. Her clothes hung from her as though she had lost a great amount of weight. Her skin was so pale it looked like she had not seen the light of day for months, and she had bruises that certainly had not come from a single beating. But what had changed the most was her demeanor. She was not the confident, arrogant girl she once had been, but a frightened young woman bowing to the one she once had hated.

"Yes, probably the last person you expect to be telling you the inner workings of Callise's dominion," said Leara.

"Yes, just about. Leara, what happened to you?" asked Rakkarah.

"Where do I begin? Well, I guess it began when I left training. I had trained two years under the council's rule when Callise came to me. I was almost sixteen, and she offered to train me so I could join the fight more quickly. For a while, everything was great. I was happy. I could do anything I pleased, as long as it didn't interfere with the war. It was like I had the world in my hands, and nothing could control me."

Her voice became dead with the next words she spoke. "But then...things started changing. It was getting close to the time when I would begin to battle. I was a good fighter, but not good enough to beat many who might challenge me. Recruiting for the dark army has become difficult these past few years. It was then that Callise saw a different use for me and many others. She decided that if we couldn't find warriors, we'd make them. She took all the unmarried women who could have children and assigned them a spouse. Only high-ranking female warriors were exempt, women like Alena. Have you all not wondered why so few dark witches are challenging any of you? They don't want to battle unless it's necessary. I was given a husband like the rest, and we started trying to have a child, as Callise wanted. I wanted her to be proud of me, to show her I was good for something. I became pregnant, but after four months, I miscarried the child. My husband's anger was overwhelming, and I was beaten often. He said it was an embarrassment not to be able to present his child to Callise. I went to Callise thinking she would help me. She helped me realize what a fool I have been. She told me his beating wasn't right, but we all have to make sacrifices in this war. She said to do what I was supposed to do, have children, and his reasons for beating me would be gone. She was not the caring woman to whom I had sworn my allegiance. I saw her as she really was: cold and heartless. I realized that I had to get out, and here was my way. I saw how wonderful your way of life looked. I saw that something was protecting and helping you that was not helping us. Really, I should say 'someone': the God I mocked. I wish I had followed Him like you; then He might have protected me," said Leara. She was crying into her hands, overcome by emotion. Rakkarah knew she was sincere; reading people was something she did well. She sat down beside Leara and took her hands.

"He can protect you now," said Rakkarah.

"I am beyond redemption. How can He forgive me, knowing the person I was? Nothing I can do could earn that forgiveness," said Leara.

"His forgiveness is not earned. If it was, no one would be forgiven. No one is so far gone that He will not accept them. He will forgive you because He loves you, just as He forgave me because He loves me. All you have you do is ask," said Rakkarah. They talked and prayed for a long time, and when they raised their heads, Leara had received her salvation. Rakkarah let the others into the room.

"I'll tell you everything I can while I am still here," said Leara.

"Still here? What do you mean?" asked Rakkarah.

"I am a trained warrior, and I have changed sides. I will be challenged, and I am not good enough to beat a great warrior. And they will send one. I will be dead within a month," said Leara.

"No you won't, because I am going to train you," said Rakkarah.

"And I'll help," said Damon. Rakkarah smiled at him. It was not in his nature to forgive easily, but seeing what they had just seen would make anyone want to help this girl.

"Thank you. Especially since I am in need of two types of training," said Leara, who knew she was in need of both training for war and for spirit.

"Miya can help with that," said Rakkarah. Miya smiled and nodded. They talked with Leara for a long time about Callise.

"Can you tell us about any unknowns, their identities?" asked Larson. Most warriors' identities where known, but there where a few who were a complete secret.

"No, Callise never reveals who they are. She has them live separate from the rest of us so no one finds out accidentally. There is actually an unknown on the high court," said Leara.

"High court?" asked Miranda.

"It's the dark form of the council, Callise and ten other," Leara explained.

"And you've never found out who it is?" asked Rakkarah.

"Never. We don't even know if it's a man or a woman. Most of us think it's a man because there are five women and four men, then the unknown. We assume she kept it even," said Leara.

"What has she been plotting?" asked Larson.

"Well, no one has dared ever say it, but I think Callise is getting scared of Rakkarah. She's constantly trying to find ways to get you. Have you noticed you've been getting more and more challenges? She's going to try sending someone who you think is weak, so you might get complacent. Then she's going to try sending someone extremely threatening, even off the high court, so you might be so scared you mess up. You are going to be getting many more battles very soon," said Leara. At these words, Miranda grabbed her brother's arm for support. It was exactly as she had thought: the war was going to spiral to a quick end.

Chapter Six:
Ghosts from the Past

Over the next few days, Rakkarah, Damon, and Miya began getting to know Leara. Her training was going better then anyone could have hoped. The best part of it all was Leara's attitude. The day after her questioning, she told them that however long she spent training for war, she would spend double that time on God. They talked more about her life in the dark order as well.

"Hey Leara, do you mind if I ask you something?" asked Rakkarah.

"Sure, anything," said Leara.

"Who was your...husband?" Rakkarah asked tentatively. Leara looked at her for a moment, then with a sad smile, she answered.

"Jayden Ross," she said. She watched looks of shock come over each of their faces.

"Jayden? But he was your best friend. How could he beat you like he did?" asked Damon. He never could imagine raising his hand to Rakkarah.

"I know he was. I thought I had gotten lucky when Callise paired us up. He was four years older than me and had been in the war longer, so I thought I could learn from him. He had always been a big part of my life, but he wasn't the Jayden I knew. When his brother Jared died a few years ago in a raid, he never got over it. He immersed himself in the war, and he hated anything that tarnished his image with Callise. After Jared died, he started drinking. That was when he'd beat me. After he'd sober up, he'd come and apologize, but things never changed," said Leara. Even though she was angry with Jayden, she couldn't help remember the way things used to be.

Hearing Leara speak, Rakkarah and her friends were reminded that, just as they did, the dark witches and wizards had friends, family, and emotions. They had people they cared for, and they felt just as they did. Sometimes that was hard to remember.

"I'm sorry that happened to you," said Rakkarah.

"I'm not. If it hadn't, I never would have left the dark side," said Leara.

After six weeks of training Leara, Rakkarah was released to go back into battle. Therefore it was no surprise that one day when the four of them went to talk to Larson, Brice burst through the door.

"There has been a challenge," said Brice.

"When do I go in?" asked Rakkarah.

"Not you...Leara," he said.

"Who challenged her?" asked Miya.

"Jayden," he said sadly.

"I could have guessed," Leara said. She was not surprised, but she was hurt. Rakkarah and Miya hugged her.

"You'll do great," said Miya.

"You've done awesome in training," said Damon.

"I had awesome trainers," said Leara.

Later that day, Miya and Rakkarah helped Leara get ready for the battle.

"So, do you know what your terms are going to be?" asked Miya.

"Yes...life. I was going to say powers—just take his power and let him live—but something changed my mind," said Leara.

"What?" asked Rakkarah.

"Do you remember what we read today? About if your eye offends you, to cast it away? I realized that Jayden caused me to do a lot of things. He was like my eyes. He was the one who made me want to join the dark witches so badly. I realized that even without his powers, he's still in a position to manipulate me. It was like only removing one eye; I can still see with the other. Anything that could tempt me back to my old ways can't be in my life anymore," said Leara.

"You're doing really well. It sounds like you've been a Christian for years," said Damon, who had been sitting by the window.

"I think, in a way, I was. When things went wrong, I'd talk to someone who wasn't there. Now I realize I was talking to God," she said, smiling.

"Maybe we should pray before we go," said Rakkarah.

"Good idea. I'll do it," said Leara. The four of them stood in a circle and joined hands. Then Leara began to pray.

"Father, this is the first time I will fight as a member of your army. I know I have a lot of time to make up for. I ask you to guide and protect me in this battle. But if I do die today, I am not afraid, because I know I will come to you. Please help me help the people that I have left, and let them see that you are the way. Let me be an example to them that you will always defeat evil. Amen," Just as she finished, Miranda knocked.

"It's time," said Miranda. They walked into the battle room. Rakkarah, Damon, and Miya stood on the sidelines as Leara walked to the center to face her husband. The mediator stepped forward.

"The battle of Jayden Ross and Leara Ross. Please state the terms, Leara," he said.

"Life," said Leara. The mediator began to speak again but was cut off by Jayden.

"Bad choice, Leara. I'll give you one chance to come back," said Jayden.

"No, I'll give you one chance to leave the dark army. Being here has changed my life. I'll never go back," said Leara.

"Never," said Jayden.

"Perform the agreement," said the mediator, before they could argue further. They raised their wands and said, "Agreed." The mediator stepped back and yelled, "Battle!" They began the battle—the most talkative battle in anyone's memory. They were casting spells and having a yelling match at the same time. It actually was quite impressive.

"If God is so real, then why did He let you lose the baby? Why would you serve someone who did that?" asked Jayden as he cast a spell.

"He wouldn't want me bringing a child into the earthly equivalent of hell," she said, blocking Jayden's spell, then casting one of the own.

"What happened to you?" asked Jayden.

"You. You beat the truth into me," she said, her next spell landing.

"Apparently, I didn't hit you hard enough," said Jayden. Walking over to her, he slapped her. She fell to the ground, but when she got up, it was with purpose.

"I hope you enjoyed that, because that was the last time!" she said. She brought her wand down over her head and yelled, "Lifera exitus!" It was done. The final thread connecting Leara to her old life was broken. After a moment of stunned silence, applause broke out. Jayden's body was given to the four who had come with him, and they left with looks of disbelief on their faces. It was then that Rakkarah stepped up to speak.

"We have seen today what I hope you all recognize as the ultimate show of faith. It is hard enough for you to risk your life for something you understand, but it is much harder to do it for something you know little about. When you go toward something knowing it is the right thing, but not knowing what will happen when you get there, it is a demonstration of the strongest faith. Look at what has happened today, and let it strengthen you as well," said Rakkarah.

The next month was fairly uneventful. Rakkarah had six battles, and Damon had three. Two other women from the dark army had come to them after hearing what had happened to Leara. They too had been forced into marriages. One of the women brought a child that was barely six months old, while the other had yet to deliver. They came with the hope of keeping their children out of the war, and they, like Leara, also had seen the power of God, although they did not understand it. Everyone was fairly calm, except Rakkarah, who had started to have strange dreams. She told no one about them. She didn't even know if you could call them dreams; they were more like random flashes of memories. She couldn't help but think that these memories were held together by a common thread, although she did not know what it was.

After a fairly uneventful day, Rakkarah went to bed, and once again she saw a stream of memories. She was nine. Her father was waking her up and taking her and her mother to a safe house. A raid was happening. That memory was cut off by a new one. She was twelve, sitting in the study of the mansion with her grandfather. He told her he loved her and not to be scared. This was the moment before he battled Warren. She held on to him for as long as she could, just in case she never got to again. This was the last time she had seen him alive. Now she was fourteen, being called out of her training class. Her father was trying to control his tears as he told her that her mother was gone.

A knock on the door caused her to jerk awake. She walked over and opened the door. A young woman stood holding an envelope. "This just arrived for you, Princess," she said. She handed the envelope to Rakkarah, then turned and walked away.

"Thank you," said Rakkarah. She walked over and sat at her window seat, looking curiously at the envelope. It looked several years old; its corners were bent, and the paper had yellowed slightly. She opened it carefully and pulled out a letter. She could not believe what she read:

My dearest granddaughter,

If this letter has made it into your hands, then two things have happene:, you have been named princess, and I am with the Lord. I have thought for a while that you might be the one, so I wrote this and left instruction to give it to you only if you had been named princess and after you turned eighteen. I wish I could be with you to help you bear this burden, but God has made other plans. I want you to know I am looking down at you now and always, and I never have left your side. You are the greatest joy in my life, and you are now the hope of our people. Rakkarah, do not try to face this alone. You have people all around you who can help you. I know Larson is taking good care of you in my absence. You are always so determined to take care of everyone else, but you never will let anyone help you.

There will be times when you will need to. You have taught me so much about life. I can't believe that so much power radiates from one little girl, though now as I look down at you, you are an even more powerful young woman. I will not write to you about the prophecy in fear of revealing what you might not know, but I want to give you a piece of advice: To see how to defeat your enemy, all you must do is use your eyes. There is a piece of the prophecy that the council does not understand, but if I am right in thinking that it is you, I understand it now. I love you more then you will ever know, and I will see you soon.

Love, Grandpa

Rakkarah stared at the letter, tears falling down her face. But they were not the sad tears that she cried when she usually thought of him. There was something about her grandfather having known she was the one that gave her comfort.

She continued to stare at the letter as she thought, "I have no idea how he knew, but he did. He always had a way of knowing who would become a great warrior, and he was the person whose judgment I trusted completely. This letter gives me more courage then I ever have known. He reminded me of something I seem to have forgotten lately: He is always with me. When I step up to Callise, I will have the greatest warrior I know by my side. Really, I will have two: my grandfather and the one he went to be with."

She looked out the window and stared into the sky.

"I love you, too," she whispered.

Chapter Seven:
Secrets

As the days wore on, battles came and went, and meetings never ended. It was amazing how mundane a war could become, but a promising night was on the horizon. Once a year, everyone who was involved in the war would come to a formal party at the mansion. It was the one night of the year when they didn't have to think about war. To most, the moments spent planning for the occasion were happy ones. The only people who took a grim outlook on the day were the council members, who remembered that the date of the party coincided with the time when the last battle probably would be fought. They all secretly wondered whether Rakkarah would live to see the day of happiness.

It was now three months until the party, and more and more battles were being lined up. Twenty-five of the twenty-eight remaining battles already were scheduled. Just as Brice had said, the letter from Rakkarah's grandfather had given her a new vigor in battle. She fought as though she were the wind moving aside leaves in her path. Her mind was at ease, and she was enjoying the time she spent with Miya and Leara preparing for the annual party.

Most people would think a constant stream of battles would wear anyone to the breaking point, but for Rakkarah, it was the exact opposite. Frequent battles kept her alert, and she gained confidence with each battle she fought. In fact, all of them were fighting well. In the past two months they had lost only six warriors; Rakkarah alone had killed almost three times as many dark warriors.

"I can't believe we have only three months," said Miya. She, Rakkarah, and Leara were all sitting in Rakkarah's room.

"There's still a lot to do. I finally get to plan something that doesn't involve fighting," said Rakkarah.

"Enjoy it while it lasts. Where's Damon?" asked Leara.

"I really don't know. He left in a hurry; he seemed like he didn't want me to know," said Rakkarah, laughing.

"That's odd," replied Miya.

"Yeah, but oh well. I just hope he's back in time for my battle," said Rakkarah. She was having yet another battle tonight with one of those unchallenging warriors Leara had talked about all those months ago.

Damon arrived half an hour before the battle with a mysterious look on his face. When they asked where he had gone, he simply smiled and said they'd know soon.

Battling had become so trivial these days that Rakkarah didn't even feel the need to be alone before them anymore. They all sat in her room until Miranda and Larson came to get them.

The battle went off without any problem; it lasted only five minutes. As everyone stood around talking afterwards, Rakkarah noticed Damon in whispered conversation with her father and Larson.

"I think he's up to something," said Miya, making the other two laugh. Damon approached and looked at the girls suspiciously.

"What's so entertaining?" he asked, smiling.

"You're not the only one who keeps secrets," said Rakkarah jokingly.

"Okay, I get it," he said.

As they stood and talked, Rakkarah slipped into her own thoughts: "Amazing what seven months has changed. An enemy has become a good friend, a letter has changed my whole mindset; but most of all, one person has succeeded in taking down every wall I have built. This part of my life is the only one that was left for me to decide, and it has been the best decision I have made. We expected Miya and Dad to be surprised when we told them, but they acted like we were telling them something as simple as "two and two make four." I hate that we have to keep everything hidden, but there will come a day when we won't have to. I feel foolish to care so much in such a short time; but then again, I can't remember my life without him—only his role has changed."

She was jerked from her musing by Larson. "Happy though we all are, it is getting late, and I think it is best we retire for the evening," he said. The room began to clear, and soon they were the only four left.

"See you tomorrow," said Miya.

"Goodnight," said Leara, and she and Miya left the room. Damon walked Rakkarah to her door, and when they got there, he kissed her cheek.

"Goodnight," he said.

"Goodnight," she said. He turned and walked down the hall.

She had almost shut the door when she stopped. "Damon," she said, and he stopped and turned around.

"Yeah?"

"Where'd you go today?" she asked. She knew he wouldn't answer her.

"You'll find out soon," he said with a smile that she couldn't quite interpret.

"Alright," she said, knowing it would do no good to argue. She closed her door and changed for bed. Damon made his way to the meeting hall, looking more nervous with each step. He emerged an hour later looking like the happiest person in the world.

The next day held a bit of a surprise: Leara was injured in a battle, but had walked away the victor.

"That's a pretty big gash," said Damon, sitting in Leara's room with the rest as the doctor tended to her wound.

"It's not that bad. I didn't even realize it was there while I was fighting," said Leara.

"That happens to me, too. I guess it's natural," said Rakkarah.

"I think a wall could fall on you while you were fighting, and you wouldn't know it," said Damon. "I remember two years ago she was in a battle and dislocated her shoulder. She finished the battle and walked out of the ring. When we told her what had happened, she looked down and said, 'Did I really?'" said Damon to the others.

"That sounds like Kar," said Miya.

"Well, it felt fine to me," said Rakkarah. They all laughed as the doctor spoke.

"You don't have to tell me. I've had to patch up the princess here more than any two warriors combined. How many battles do you have coming up?" he asked Rakkarah.

"Twenty-three scheduled before the party. I've actually got one tonight," she said to him.

"You would think Callise would tire of having her warriors killed off," he said with a smile of confidence.

"I'm sure she's getting there," said Rakkarah. She said it jokingly, but in her head, she knew it was the complete truth.

"Leara, make sure you keep medication on that cut. It should heal in about a week," said the doctor.

Chapter Eight:
The Fiftieth Battle

The next two months were busier than the previous two, inside the war and out. Rakkarah had fought twenty of her twenty-three battles with nothing more serious than some cuts and a sprained wrist. In the way of non-war issues, things were far less simple. Planning for the party consumed many hours of the day. Three weeks before the party, Rakkarah, Miya, and Leara all had to have final alterations to their dresses.

"I really don't see why they insist on my entering like it's such a big deal. Everyone in that room has seen me before," said Rakkarah. The other two laughed. They knew things like that annoyed Rakkarah; she liked simplicity.

"Kar, you're their leader. They think everything you do is a big deal," said Miya.

"Yeah, watching me try not to fall in heels is truly a sight to behold," said Rakkarah, laughing.

"You can't wear those boots you wear in battle with everything," said Leara.

"I don't see why not. You can't see my feet in this," said Rakkarah, indicating the long, puffy skirt of her dress. They spent a few more minutes joking, when Damon entered the room.

"Damon, will you please tell Kar that her boots are not okay to wear with her dress?" asked Miya.

"I don't see why not. You can't see her feet in that," he said.

"I think you two share one mind; she just said that exact thing," said Leara.

They finished thirty minutes later and left for the study, where they found William, Larson, and Miranda waiting for them.

"How many battles do you have coming up, Kar?" asked her father.

"Three: one tomorrow, one Wednesday, and one Thursday," said Rakkarah.

"And one Saturday and Monday if you accept them," said Brice as he entered the room. "The challenges just came," he added.

"Alright, is it anyone powerful?" she asked.

"Not pushovers, but nothing for you. The worst is Anthony Mitchell," said Brice. The way he said it, no one noticed the anxiousness that penetrated his mind. As he looked at Miranda, he saw they hid their feelings just as well as he did, but each knew what the other was thinking. They all shared the same thought: one challenge and two signs to go.

As they expected, all five of Rakkarah's battles came and went, but the council still waited with baited breath. Larson, Miranda, and Brice were spending much of their free time in the meeting hall talking it over.

"It's less than two weeks until the party, and she has only one battle left. I can't believe it," said Brice.

"We still have the signs left," said Miranda.

"When that battle happens, those signs will come faster than we can see them," said Larson.

"How do you know that?" asked Miranda.

"I just know. This next battle before she goes against Callise will be monumental. I can feel it. I can almost see the whites of Callise's eyes," said Larson.

"He's right. Callise is so close, I can feel her stepping on my heels, breathing down my neck. She haunts me like an unrelenting storm," said Brice.

"What do we do?" asked Miranda.

"Pray," said Larson. They bowed their heads, and Larson spoke to God as he never had done in the presence of others.

"My Lord, we stand here on the edge of an abyss. We are helpless to stop the task you have set at our girl's feet, but we ask that you take her hand and guide her as we can't. We know you never would allow your Word to be taken from our hands, but we know that should we lose Rakkarah, that is what will happen. My Lord, you've sent us a savior for our souls, and now you've sent a savior of our lives—to many, she is life. Help her to do what all others have failed to do in this thirty-year rage. Lord, the next sign to be shown is a haunting vision from the past. I do not know what it is, but I ask that it will make her stronger, not rip her apart. If there were a way I could take her place, I would not hesitate, but I know that is not your will, so allow me to take any pain away from her that I can. Lord, I also ask that you bless these next few days, for what is coming will bring her more happiness then she has ever known. Amen."

Five days later, they were sitting in the study when, as had happened so many times before, Brice came into the room. Only this time, he did not hide his worry.

"You've been challenged, Rakkarah," he said.

"By whom?" she asked. She did not like the look on his face or the sound of his voice. It took him a moment to answer, as if he thought no one would believe him; he didn't want to believe himself. He wasn't sure if his voice would form the name, but when he spoke, his voice was clear.

"Warren," he said. They stood in slience for several moments. No one knew what to say to Rakkarah. What do you say to someone who just found out that the man who killed her grandfather is going to try to do the same to her? They each were having different emotions about the battle. William was horror struck. Miya was almost crying. Leara felt a mix of shock and fear. Damon felt rage course through him as he had never felt before. The only ones who were not surprised were Rakkarah and Larson. Larson had figured on a sinister last battle, and Rakkarah always had known the day would come when she would have to face her grandfather's killer. Finally, Brice spoke.

"Do you accept?" he asked.

"Yes," she said. "When?"

"In an hour," said Brice. For a few seconds, they all stood motionless. But then Rakkarah walked as quickly as she could from the room and didn't stop until she arrived at her chambers. She walked over to her wardrobe and pulled out her battle clothes, but instead of putting them on, she threw them on her bed. She stood by her window looking at the setting sun as a few tears fell from her eyes. It was then she felt a hand on her shoulder.

Chapter Nine:
Time to Know the Enemy

"You're ready to face him," said Damon.

"I can wait a thousand years, and I still won't be ready," she replied.

"He's nothing. He can't defeat anyone without trickery," said Damon.

"He killed the greatest warrior I know," said Rakkarah, now turning to face him.

"But he only killed the second greatest warrior I know," said Damon. At that point, Rakkarah let her weakness show.

"I'm scared, Damon," she said. She never had admitted this to anyone. He held her tightly, thinking he would rather do anything than admit that he was—if it was possible—even more afraid than she was. He was scared every time she walked into the ring, every time he said goodbye to her, knowing it could be the last time he spoke to her, and knowing he should tell her everything.

After several minutes, Rakkarah stopped crying and went to change for the battle. It was ten minutes until time, when Damon saw Warren and the other dark warriors walking toward the mansion. Rakkarah stood by his side and stared down at them as well. As she looked down at Warren, she knew.

"You're right, I am ready," she said, looking up at Damon. He smiled at her.

"You always have been," he said. They stood there until the knock on the door came. Rakkarah began to walk toward the door, but Damon caught her by the hand.

"I love you, Kar," he said. Looking into his eyes, she knew it was true, and she knew that she did, too.

"I love you, too," she said.

The walk down the hall had to be one of the longest she ever had endured, but her mind had switched over.

"I know I can't defeat Warren on fighting ability alone because he is too skilled," she thought. "I have to play to his weakness. I can't deny either that a surprise death spell in battle is not enough to satisfy me. I want him to know his death is coming, and I want him to know he is powerless to stop it. I want to see fear shine in his eyes. What I will do has not been done before, but I think it's time for a change of pace."

They stopped outside the double doors, and Rakkarah bowed her head to pray before they opened. She knew this was the time she needed it the most. The doors opened to the usual sight, but to Rakkarah, it was a completely different scene. She saw Warren standing in the middle of the ring. She walked forward, knowing what she had to do. Usually the room would be buzzing with whispered conversations, but tonight, all was silent. Everyone knew this would be the fiercest battle they ever had seen. They could tell by the fire in their princess's eyes. When she stepped into the ring, she looked Warren in the eyes for the first time, and for an instant, the fire seemed to have broken free. Several gasped, but they knew it must have been a trick of the light.

Whatever reaction Warren had expected, this was not it. The girl before him knew no fear and would show no mercy. Before the mediator could step forward, Warren spoke to Rakkarah.

"Ready to die like your grandfather, little girl?" he asked. To his surprise, she gave a small laugh. "You find his death funny? Odd way to show your love for him," he continued in an amused voice.

"No, I find it funny that a grown man feels the need to intimidate a nineteen-year-old girl. What's the matter, you couldn't find anyone to throw a cheap shot? You're really losing your edge," said Rakkarah, sometimes looking at him, sometimes casting her gaze around the room to show him she was not worried in the least. As she had hoped, this made him extremely angry.

"Playing around in battle isn't smart, and neither is shooting your mouth off. I killed your greatest warrior, the leader before you. What do you have to back up your words, a bunch of unimportant recruits?" he said to her in a heated voice. Rakkarah again dismissed his words.

"You know, for someone who loves to hear himself talk as much as you do, you'd figure you'd at least know what you're talking about. As for all of those pushover warriors, if Callise wants to send them into obvious death, that's her business. Tell her to send a challenging one next time. I'm getting bored. The only problem is you won't make it back to tell her," said Rakkarah. She knew she had done it; he was enraged. As she had said all those months ago, the worst thing to do was fight out of emotion, and that was exactly what she was going to make him do.

"Can we begin now?" said Rakkarah. The mediator stepped forward.

"The battle of Princess Rakkarah and Warren Newman. The terms will be set by the Princess. State them now," he said. Standing and looking into Warren's eyes, she shot him one more firey stare and then answered to the entire room.

"Life," she said.

"Bad choice," said Warren.

"For you," said Rakkarah.

"Please perform the agreement," said the mediator. They extended their wands.

"Agreed," they said in unison, and then stood at ready.

"Battle!" yelled the mediator.

Rakkarah landed the first spell, causing Warren to stumble several paces backward. Warren retaliated, sending a spell that caused Rakkarah to fall to the ground. The spells flashed continually. Warren had cuts across his face, while Rakkarah's shoulder was badly bruised and her side was grazed. Then a powerful spell from Warren knocked Rakkarah on her back. She let out a moan of pain, and Warren stood over her.

"It's all over," said Warren as he raised his wand to cast a death spell.

"Not quite," said Rakkarah. She suddenly kicked her leg up and caused Warren's wand to fly from his hand. Warren dove for his wand, but when he reached it, he found it broken.

Rakkarah was back on her feet. Warren turned to face her. She cast a single spell that knocked him down. There was a bright flash of light, and when everyone looked around, Rakkarah had vanished.

"Where'd she go? Where'd she go?" Warren screamed, spinning around and looking for Rakkarah. Rakkarah dropped to her feet behind him. When he turned around, he found her two feet from his face. He barely had time to register what he was seeing when a well-aimed kick put him back on his knees. She walked around behind him, and he leaned his head back to look at her.

"It's not smart to shoot your mouth off in a battle. If you just had cast the spell, you might have beaten me," said Rakkarah. She looked into his eyes and saw that he knew he was finished. She grasped his chin and one side of his head, and with one swift movement and bone-chilling crack, Warren fell limply to the floor.

Rakkarah looked around the room at everyone's shocked faces. It was a few minutes before anyone spoke.

"You can't do that!" said one of the dark warriors.

"I just did," said Rakkarah.

"That can't be legal," said another dark wizard.

"It is; nothing prohibits physical maneuvers," said the mediator.

"I actually think it was more fair. I mean, his wand was broken, so he couldn't use magic. I put my wand away. He and I were on equal ground. He could have defended himself," said Rakkarah. The dark warriors could not argue with that truth; she'd had nothing he hadn't. They accepted Warren's body and left. Everyone stood amazed at Rakkarah's unique victory. No one seemed sure what to say, until one man spoke.

"So, when do we start training for that?" he asked. Everyone laughed, and discussions broke out over the room about Rakkarah's battle. As everyone began to leave, Rakkarah pulled Larson aside.

"I want to talk to you," she whispered.

"I'll be in the meeting hall," he replied. Rakkarah turned to Damon.

"I'll be back in my room in about an hour," she said, and turned and left the room. She arrived in the meeting hall a few minutes later to find Larson sitting at the table waiting for her.

"Congratulations. That was amazing. You played to his every weakness," he said with a smile.

"Thanks. I hope no one else tries that; I'm afraid I started something," she said with a small laugh.

"What did you want to talk to me about, Kar?" he asked.

"I want to know about Callise, everything about her," she replied. Larson looked at her appraisingly.

"Why?" he asked curiously, raising his eyebrow.

"I realized something right after I killed Warren. I won because...After he killed my grandfather, I found out everything I could about him. I knew what he could not defend against; I knew magic alone wouldn't work. I know so much of him and so little of her. She could challenge me any day, and I'm walking into the ring with my eyes closed; I'm blind to her. For all the power Warren had, Callise has double. My purpose is to fight her, but I have no idea what I'm fighting," she said. Larson had noticed how she had paused and her voice had broken when she mentioned her grandfather. He couldn't help but be amazed at her wisdom, for she was correct that knowing her enemy was the best path to victory.

She sat down beside him and waited. Larson took a deep breath and then began.

"Well, I knew Callise fairly well when she was younger. I was grown when she was in training. She was always determined, did anything she set her mind to. People liked that about her. She always was a nice girl. She had only one flaw: she didn't like authority; she wanted to be free. She was as impossible to tame as the wind. She was God-worshipping, like the rest of us, but seemed reluctant to give even Him complete control. She always did everything she was supposed to, but something happened that changed all of that," At this point Larson stopped, reflecting on the memory.

"What happened?" asked Rakkarah, bewildered.

"She fell in love," said Larson.

"What?" asked Rakkarah.

"She had been best friends with a boy named Marshall since childhood. As time passed, their relationship developed, not very different from you and Damon. I don't think you could have found two people who loved each other more. Before too long they were engaged," said Larson, stopping again. Rakkarah wished he would quit pausing. She was growing more confused by the second.

"How could love make her like that?" she asked.

"Marshall was almost as untamable as Callise. He was a good guy, but he liked to do things his way. He never backed down from anything. One night Marshall and Callise went into the city, and this man, a mortal, started a fight with Marshall. They began to argue, then push, and then punch. Marshall knew it was against our law to use magic on another, so he never drew his wand. Marshall punched the guy so hard once that he fell to the ground. When he got up, there was a knife in his hand. He stabbed Marshall through the heart, and he died almost instantly. The man was put in jail, but that wasn't enough for Callise. She stayed shut away for two months not talking to anybody. One night she left her house and used illegal magic to sneak into the prison where Marshall's killer was kept. He became the first victim of the death spell. We figured out what she had done and brought her in. She showed no remorse. She was very blunt. She said there was no God, because God would not let that happen to His people. She said no one would control her power again. We left the room to decide what to do with her, and when we came back, she had disappeared. Word got out about what Callise had done and said. It was appealing to many people, people who wanted revenge or power. Before we knew what was happening, Callise emerged with our people who had gone to her side, or mortals she offered the chance. Most people thought we'd stop the rebellion quickly, but here we are, thirty years later," explained Larson. He had gone on for a long time. Rakkarah could tell he wanted to say it all at once. She knew this memory haunted him; the ghost of the years past drifted through his strong eyes.

"Now that I know what happened, I almost feel sorry for her," said Rakkarah.

"That is one of your best and worst qualities," said Larson.

Rakkarah looked at him with an odd expression. "What do you mean?" she asked.

"What happened to her was horrible, but Callise is not to be pitied. She lost someone she loved and saw fit for thousands to die as a result. You lost two, and stand as strong as ever. I don't think she is anyone to feel sorry for," said Larson. Rakkarah knew he was right; she was now almost angry. A broken heart does not justify a thirty-year killing spree. When she looked into Larson's eyes, he saw that famous fire was back.

"Did I tell you what you needed to know?" he asked her.

"Yes. Now I know she can feel, and I know she has weakness. It's just nice to know I'm fighting a human. I've always thought of her as some sort of unflinching rock," said Rakkarah.

"I think that is how most people see her," said Larson understandingly.

"How have you done this all these years?" asked Rakkarah.

"You. I knew you were going to come and do what all others couldn't. This is the second time we've been saved from what we couldn't overcome. God sends only special people to save the world. I know of only two who have had that cursed privilege," said Larson.

"My task is nothing compared to what Jesus did," said Rakkarah.

"No, but your stories are similar. You both gave over your whole life for a people and a God you love. I can think of few who would do that," said Larson.

"Thanks, Larson," she said.

"Always. Now, don't worry about what's going to happen. There is enough to worry about in the present; don't let the future add problems," he said knowingly. She nodded, and he continued. "Even though you have to deal with the problems of someone twice your age, you are still allowed to be young." Rakkarah left a few minutes later and returned to her room to find her three friends waiting for her.

Chapter Ten:
A New Life

"Where did you go?" asked Damon.

"I went to ask Larson about Callise," she said.

"Why, don't you know all you need to?" asked Miya.

"No, not at all," said Rakkarah. She began to explain all she had talked about with Larson. "I wanted to know about her past, how she became the way she is, and who she was before that. I found out that Callise was in love, and someone killed her fiancé. She thought that if his powers had not been controlled by our law, he would have been able to save himself. She wanted the man who killed him dead, but knew the council would never do that, so she took matters into her own hands. She made the death spell, went to the jail where he was kept, and killed him. Before they could stop her, she recruited her followers, promising revenge and power, and now here we are fighting today."

"That explains a lot. We always wondered why Callise never married. We all figured she would want her own line to keep power after she passed, but she had no heirs. We all wanted to know who would claim power," said Leara.

"Didn't anyone ever ask?" asked Miya.

"No. There's an unspoken agreement between Callise and the dark warriors," said Leara.

"What's that?" asked Damon.

"Don't ask Callise questions about her life, and you don't have to worry about losing yours. Of course, she doesn't kill them in front of everyone. We just wake up one day and they're gone," said Leara.

"Don't you ever ask what happened?" asked Miya.

"Not unless you want to be next," said Leara, laughing at Miya's inability to grasp this concept.

The next day the council met again.

"So, the last battle went well," said a council member.

"It was impressive. I didn't know Rakkarah had that up her sleeve," said Brice.

"It was impressive, but for now we have two signs to worry about," said Miranda.

"It doesn't help we have no idea what one of them means: 'When fire burns to its full blaze.' I can't make heads or tails of it," said Brice.

"Again, that one is not my concern; this thing from the past is. We can put out a fire; we can't destroy history," said Larson.

"I'll bet anything Callise controls that sign. Every bad thing in Rakkarah's life has happened because of Callise, and Callise will want to use it to try to weaken Rakkarah. But it very well could work to Kar's advantage. She always channels her feelings into power, so this might give her more," said Brice.

"I'm not worried about what it does to her in the battle. We have to think about what she will go through after. What if this haunts her for the rest of her life?" asked Miranda.

"She's strong. Whatever it is will affect her for a while, but time and God will heal her," said Larson.

"Well, let's not worry about it until after the party. I really don't think it will happen until it's over," said Brice.

The morning of the party dawned to great excitement. Everyone rose early to help with the preparations. They spent the morning moving in tables and decorations. By three o'clock, the ballroom was gleaming with beauty. Everyone was due to arrive at five, and Rakkarah would enter at five forty-five. As soon as they had finished the ballroom, Damon again disappeared with William and Larson and then returned twenty minutes later. Rakkarah couldn't help noticing how nervous he looked, though he kept it well from everyone but her. Soon after, everyone went upstairs to get ready. Rakkarah and the other two girls were getting dressed in her room.

"Did either of you notice Damon leave with Larson and my dad?' asked Rakkarah.

"Oh yeah, I was wondering about that," said Leara, adjusting her emerald-green dress.

"He has been acting odd all day. I wonder what's bothering him," said Rakkarah.

"It's probably nothing," said Miya, standing in front of the mirror in her lavender dress. Miranda entered the room at this moment.

"Miya, Leara, it's four forty-five; you're supposed to come down early," said Miranda.

"Alright. Bye, Kar," said Miya.

"See you soon," said Leara.

Rakkarah stood up and walked over to the mirror. She was wearing a dark purple dress patterned with black lace, with black gloves that came to her elbows. Her hair was pulled up with soft curls falling around her face. No more than five minutes after the girls had left, Damon knocked and entered the room.

"Hey," she said as he walked toward her. "Aren't you supposed to be downstairs with everyone else?"

"No, I asked Larson and your dad for time to talk to you before," he said, as if not wanting to give too much away.

"Am I about to find out what the mysterious meetings with them are about?" she said chidingly.

"Yes, and where I went a while back—I told you I'd tell you eventually," he said with a smile. As nervous as he was, he couldn't help being amazed at how beautiful she looked. Even though he had no idea what to say, he began to talk.

"Kar...I know you have a lot going on with the war right now, and I know keeping our relationship a secret is important to you, but I want you to know I'm not afraid of anything Callise will do. We can't put our lives on hold until this war ends. That could be twenty years from now. I know a lot of your life has been chosen for you, but it is your life, and some things you can choose for yourself. What happens with us is your decision," said Damon.

While he was talking, he had taken her hand, and when she looked down, a ring was there that had not been there before. She looked back at him, speechless.

"It's time to decide," he said to her. For a moment, her mind told her that to say yes was the greatest danger she could put him in. But her mind was quickly drowned out by a stronger force. Everything he had said was true. She could not wait for this war to end to live her life. If she did, she might never have a life. This war was going to control her life no longer.

"Yes," she said, as he hugged her tightly. "So my dad and Larson already know?" she asked.

"They and Miranda. I had to get her to get Miya and Leara out of the way early," he said to her.

"When did you tell them?" she asked.

"The day I left and didn't tell you where I was going, I asked your dad right after we left the battle hall. None of them really were surprised. It's like they suspected it," he said.

"Miya and Leara are going to be mad you didn't tell them what you were doing," said Rakkarah chidingly.

"I told Miranda she could tell them after they left," he said. "We'd better go. I told your dad we'd come down to the meeting hall afterwards. He wanted to see you before the ball," he said.

They walked down to the meeting hall and found quite a few people waiting for them. William, Larson, Miranda, Miya, and Leara were all waiting eagerly around the room. Rakkarah's father walked toward her, though he didn't know what to say. After she hugged him, he found his voice.

"I'm happy for you, Kar," he said smiling.

"Thanks, Dad," she said. A moment later, Miya and Leara, unable to restrain themselves any longer, ran over and hugged both Rakkarah and Damon. Larson and Miranda then came over to congratulate them.

"I'm proud; you're finally doing something for you," Larson said to Rakkarah. While they were all still in conversation, Brice knocked on the door.

"Five minutes until your entrance, Kar. What's everyone doing in here?" he asked, staring at the crowd gathered there.

"We'll tell you in the ballroom," said Rakkarah.

They all walked out of the room and made their way to the ballroom. The rest went in, but Rakkarah stayed behind the closed double doors. She stood there waiting and thinking, "This is always the best day of the year, and until today, I didn't think it could be better. That just shows how wrong I can be. Suddenly all of my obstacles feel like nothing, and I feel for the first time in my life I am ready to face Callise and all her horrors when the times comes."

The doors opened, and Rakkarah walked in to loud clapping and cheering. After she greeted the people, the celebration commenced.

An hour into the festivities, Larson asked Rakkarah the question he had wanted to ask all night: "So, will the engagement be another secret, or are you planning an announcement?"

Rakkarah looked at Damon, and they seemed to know the obvious choice. "I'm tired of secrets; we'll announce it before the end of the night," said Rakkarah.

"I still can't believe you're—" began Miya, but she stopped when the doors suddenly burst open. Five people came through the doors; in the lead was a woman with blonde hair. At the sight of her, most people backed away, and some screamed. It was not without reason. This woman was Callise.

Chapter Eleven:
The Final Battle

"Ready for your last battle, Princess?" she asked.

"Yes, are you?" Rakkarah replied.

"You know it doesn't have to be like this, Rakkarah. I don't want to kill you. You are a very powerful witch. Think of what you could do with your powers if they were not restrained by anything. If you would open your eyes to your potential, you could find a place of high esteem among my ranks," said Callise.

"The thought of what I could do with my powers sickens me, as it should you," said Rakkarah.

"You just don't understand, do you? My people use their powers without shame or fear. Everyone desires freedom—even you. I can see it," said Callise.

"It seems to me that some are ashamed. Why else would one of your warriors come here with their face covered?" asked Rakkarah, indicating a warrior behind Callise wearing a long, black hood.

"She doesn't do it on her will; she does it because I ask. But maybe it might be better for her to show herself. If anyone, she can show you the good of my way. I believe you know her well," said Callise. Everyone could see she wanted to reveal the mystery woman. She brought the woman up beside her. The woman hesitated a second, lifted her hands, and removed her covering. She was a pretty woman with light brown hair. When Rakkarah saw her, she almost fell to the ground.

"Rakkarah," said the woman.

"Mom?" asked Rakkarah.

"Isabella?" said William.

"Yes, William," said Isabella.

"Mom, what's going on? I thought you were dead," said Rakkarah.

"No, I'm sorry for what happened. This wasn't how I meant for things to happen. I planned to come back for you a few months after I left. I was going to bring you to train under Callise, but after you became the princess, I knew I couldn't," said Isabella.

"You couldn't have anyway. I know where my loyalty lies," said Rakkarah, displaying a mixture of anger and disbelief.

"Kar, it's a wonderful life. No one tells you how to live, especially not some God that we've never even seen. It is complete freedom," said Isabella.

"Does freedom include Callise arranging my marriage and throwing my children into battle? If that's your idea of freedom, I don't want it," shot Rakkarah.

"Rakkarah—" began her mother.

"Be quiet, Isabella," said Rakkarah. After a long pause, her mother spoke again.

"No matter what side of this war I am on, I am still your mother, and I deserve your respect," said Isabella slowly.

"You're not my mother. My mother wouldn't abandon me. My mother never would serve the woman who killed her husband's father, and who is trying to kill me. As far as I am concerned, my mother died when I was fourteen," said Rakkarah, pulling out her wand and pointing it at Isabella. Isabella laughed.

"Come on, Rakkarah. No matter how mad at me you are, we both know you can't kill your own mother," said Isabella.

"Oh, no, I could, but killing you isn't good enough for me. Poweiro remavera!" she yelled. Isabella fell to her knees, and Rakkarah stood over her.

"Since you love her so much more than me, you can watch her die," said Rakkarah. Rakkarah saw her mother was very weak, which was to be expected. Rakkarah had taken her mother's powers. Now she turned to Callise, her fiery eyes ablaze again.

"So do we agree on life, then?" asked Rakkarah.

"Yes, I think so," said Callise.

"We need a mediator," said Rakkarah.

"I'll do it," said Larson, and he stepped forward.

"This is the battle of Princess Rakkarah and Callise. The terms are life. The formal agreement is to be performed now." He paused to allow Rakkarah and Callise to extend their wands and say, "Agreed," then he continued. "Everything is allowed. There can be no outside interference. The battle will begin on my say." He paused and looked into Rakkarah's eyes. It was then he suddenly understood. He nodded to her, and then yelled, "Battle!"

It was battling as they had never seen before. Spells shot by so fast, it was difficult to discern who had cast them. They were both getting hit, but neither seemed to be affected.

"Had enough, Princess?" asked Callise.

"No, haven't you? Thirty years of this over one person!" said Rakkarah. Callise looked at her, astounded.

"Yeah, I know about that," said Rakkarah. At this, Callise cast a spell that caused Rakkarah to fly back ten feet and land on the floor. When she got up, she shook the hair from her eyes, and it looked as though fire were coming out of them. But—no, it really was. Fire was pouring out of Rakkarah's eyes and onto every part of her body until she was an inferno. The fire was not burning her, but people around her could feel the heat from it. Callise's eyes widened in shock, much like everyone else's, for this was a power they had never seen. Rakkarah walked slowly toward Callise. Though she was as astounded as the rest, she somehow knew exactly what she had to do. Stopping where Callise stood paralyzed with fear, Rakkarah slowly reached out her hand and, after a moment's pause, placed her hand just below Callise's throat.

Her screams echoed throughout the room. Rakkarah wanted to remove her hand, but knew she couldn't. It was time to finish this. Rakkarah heard her mother and the other dark warriors screaming, but they wouldn't come near. It seemed like it would never end. Callise was screaming in pain, but still alive. Finally, after what seemed like an eternity, Callise ceased to scream. She looked back into Rakkarah's eyes with one tear rolling down her face. She uttered one word—"Marshall"—then slumped over. Callise was dead, and the fire went out. Behind Callise, Rakkarah's mother and the other three warriors stood for a moment. One by one, they each began to fall over dead. With only Isabella still alive, she took the little strength left in her and struggled over to Rakkarah. When she was a foot away from her, her knees gave way. Rakkarah caught her before she hit the floor, and when she looked into her mother's face, it was tear-stained. Rakkarah lowered her mother to the ground, supporting her head and shoulders.

"You're right, Kar. I don't deserve your forgiveness, but I hope you will give it to me anyway. Maybe God will forgive me, too," said Isabella.

"I do, and so does He," said Rakkarah, tears falling freely from her eyes.

"And even though I didn't prove it, I hope you know I love you," said Isabella.

"I love you too, Mom," said Rakkarah. Her mother gave a slight smile before her body went limp.

As Rakkarah knelt crying beside her mother, she felt someone lift her off the ground. She opened her eyes and saw it was Damon. He just looked at her. He couldn't imagine what was going through her head.

"It's over; you freed us," said Damon.

Rakkarah stopped crying. It had not registered with her until that moment: The war was finally over. She looked around at all of her people. They were shocked, but the reality of what had just happened was sinking in. Everyone looked around for a moment, then smiles broke out over their faces. The next moment, deafening cheers broke out; everyone yelled and jumped, and some even cried. As Rakkarah celebrated with the others, she couldn't help thinking that it was the best and worst day of her life. She told herself not to worry about the bad, because God had given her too much good to celebrate. Several hours later, Larson called for silence.

"This is truly the day we have waited for, though it came with its share of heartache. It is hard to imagine making this day any happier, but there is one special announcement that needs to be made," said Larson. He turned to look at Rakkarah, but Rakkarah was looking at her father.

"Dad, will you make the announcement?" she asked him. She knew her father was hurting more than she was. He stepped forward, smiling.

"I am very happy to tell you that my daughter, your princess, is going to be married. I'm proud to say that Damon will be joining our family soon," said William. The cheers were just as loud as they had been before. The celebration didn't stop until five the next morning, and when everyone went to bed, it was with complete peace. For the next few months, no one seemed sure what to do. This was to be expected, as many had never known life without war. However, gradually people found their place in this new world.

Chapter Twelve:
Destiny

Eight months later, Rakkarah stood in front of her mirror once again, only this time for a different purpose. She gazed at her reflection in a long, white dress with a veil over her face. Gwen stood behind her arranging her dress, while Miya and Leara stood on each side of her wearing matching dresses of gold.

"You look beautiful, Kar," said Miya.

"Thanks," said Rakkarah. She looked back into the mirror engrossed in her thoughts.

"Eight months ago I stood in front of this mirror preparing for the ball, and, though I did not know it then, my battle with Callise," she thought. "It's still strange to wake up to peace, to live a day without Brice asking if I accept a challenge. For so long, I've stood in this very spot preparing to take a life, but today I stand here preparing to start a new one. God has given me the life I've always wanted, the life I thought was impossible. I pray everyday for God to continue to bless me and my people and to keep us on the right path. I pray we never forget what God helped us to overcome, and that as we walk our roads of life, we remember that war still exists within our spirits. As I begin this new life with Damon, I hope I don't worry over the petty problems of life and that I never take for granted one second of my life. I've learned to treasure every second, because it might be my last. I do not know what surprises my future holds, but I do know I welcome every one of them. And now...it's time to begin my new life."

"Ready?" asked Leara.

"Yes," she replied.

The ceremony was beautiful. All of the people came to see Rakkarah and Damon marry. Larson preformed the ceremony; he had been a minister before the war. As William watched his daughter, there was a gleam in his eye that had not been there since he had seen Isabella. After the ceremony, they all went to the reception, which was a sight to behold. Rakkarah danced with Damon and then with her father. When she threw the bouquet, Miya caught it. They all found this amusing, because Miya had been seeing an ex-warrior, a friend of Rakkarah's, seven months earlier. After several hours, Rakkarah and Damon said goodbye and left to start their new life.

Two years later, Rakkarah lay in a bed in the hospital, exhausted but overjoyed. Damon stood by her with his hand on her shoulder. On the other side of the room, a baby began to cry. A nurse came over, holding her in a soft blanket.

"Your daughter, Your Majesty," she said with a smile, gently laying the baby in Rakkarah's arms.

"She's so beautiful," said Rakkarah, who could not take her eyes off her daughter.

"Just like her mother," said Damon, also unable to look at anything else but the baby. Rakkarah extended her arms so Damon could hold her. After about ten minutes, he laid the baby back in Rakkarah's arms.

"I'll go get everyone; they'll want to see her, too," he said. He left the room. Rakkarah looked at her daughter and thought, "Thank you, God, you have given me the greatest gift I could ever ask for. I thought defeating Callise would be the biggest accomplishment of my life, but as I look at this baby, it's not even close. Who would have thought I would give birth to a baby with eyes of fire? I see them already." Rakkarah looked at her daughter and whispered, "I love you, my baby girl."

At that moment, Damon returned with William, Larson, Miranda, Miya and her husband, and Leara with her fiancé.

"Oh, she's beautiful," said Miya.

"Do you want to hold your granddaughter, Dad?" Rakkarah asked her father.

"Yes, I do," he said reaching out and lifting the baby from Rakkarah's arms. For a while, everyone took turns holding the baby. As Leara walked to Rakkarah's bed and gave the baby back to Rakkarah, she asked the question they all had been wondering.

"What's her name, Kar?" she asked.

Funny enough, she and Damon had thought of that just the night before. They wanted to give her a name with special meaning. They talked about how everything in their lives had been part of God's perfect plan. The prophecy, their relationship, the war, and even the sleeping baby in Rakkarah's arms all came down to one word, and it was the name they decided to give their daughter.

"Destiny," said Rakkarah, and Larson nodded.

"It fits," he said, then walked over and spoke to Destiny. "Destiny, if you are half as good a princess as your mother, then your future is bright," he said.

Rakkarah and Damon looked down and silently prayed that God watch over their Destiny.